P9-DYZ-476

SHEPHERD'S SWORD

Alexander Family -

May God's blessings
follow each of you
always

Dan Wilson

Rom 8:28

SHEPHERD'S SWORD

Daniel E. Wilson

Daniel E. Wilson

Copyright © 2008 **Daniel E. Wilson**

ISBN 978-1-60145-616-8

All rights reserved. No part of this publication may be reproduced, stored in a retrieval system, or transmitted in any form or by any means, electronic, mechanical, recording or otherwise, without the prior written permission of the author.

Printed in the United States of America.

The characters and events in this book are fictitious. Any similarity to real persons, living or dead, is coincidental and not intended by the author.

Booklocker.com, Inc.
2008

SHEPHERD'S SWORD

I have the great privilege to dedicate this book to my father Roy, who inspired me to dream and seek adventures in life, and to my mother Joan, who was always an encouragement and example of grace.

I am also dedicating this to my beautiful bride Robin, who somehow keeps my feet on the ground, but allows my head to sail in the clouds. I love you Honey!

TABLE OF CONTENTS:

CHAPTER 1

The Dark Night

"Why does the darkness bother me so?" Joshua puzzled as he collected water from the nearby well. His thoughts returning to past events and times he'd been forced to flee for his life, or beatings he'd received on other such dark nights as this from his old Master Cekil.

Barely into his seventeenth year, Joshua had seen and experienced more than his share of hardships and hurts. Though his life had taken a turn for the better, past experiences were hard to forget and the fear of being pulled back into the painful blackness was an ever present hound. But Joshua knew it wasn't the darkness that had him worried, but the gripping fear of losing the freedom to define his own future and control his own destiny.

Unfortunately, it wasn't always wise to do such errands during the broad daylight when others could steal his work or ask too many questions about his and his partner Japed's sheep; especially considering some of the common form of people you'd find in the valleys of southern Samaria. That's why Japed had suggested they make such late night expeditions to gather grain and straw left behind by the pickers and to make the long trek to the well of Shilo at Malik. And Joshua was more than willing to accept whatever uneasiness he'd have in order to nurture his treasured flock and recently found freedom.

Daniel E. Wilson

One thing was for certain, Joshua was not uncomfortable because of the dark itself. The day had been very hot, even in the shade, while the night was unusually comfortable with a slight breeze. It may have been the breeze itself that made him somewhat wary by its invisible and eerie movement through trees and bushes. Although the stars were as bright as ever, the lack of a moon made the walk discomfiting and slow.

Joshua thought about Hanna. How he was glad he didn't have to carry her along with him. Not that he had any hard feelings toward her, but that he knew he would have had to help her more on this night than he could afford. As the thought emerged, he felt the pang of guilt that bothered him each time he poorly considered his young friend. It wasn't Hanna's fault that she was crippled. It wasn't her fault for anything. Hanna had always made an effort to be useful when she could, and when she couldn't, she knew to stay out of the way.

As he was thinking of her, a smile came over Joshua's face. Though she was often more of a burden than anything else, Joshua thought about how she'd pressed him into allowing her to come along. She was new to her 15th year now, and sorely wanted to be of value somehow and knew that these evening excursions were the best cloak for the scars on her face and ungainly limp. So she tried as best she could to explain how she'd not be a burden and would be quiet the whole while if Joshua would take her along. How her big brown eyes pleaded to go in one instance, then pouted in the next. His smile broadened remembering how she did everything she could to help him pack the necessary items for the trek to the well. What a great heart for such a lowly creature.

It seemed as though the night would last forever, his only comfort in knowing that he could sleep in the shade tomorrow while Japed would tend the sheep. It was always his favorite things to do. Sleep during the day, where his dreams could wander to faraway lands, beautiful forests and exciting adventures. Joshua longed deeply for the carefree life. He wanted so very much to help Hanna win over her challenges, and find a doctor who could care for her legs and the scars that Shaman had left on her youthful face.

Joshua remembered the first time he met Hanna. She had been cleaning the front of her home, and her humble but carefree demeanor caused Joshua to stop and talk to her on his way to the market. Her friendly, but awkward smile only slightly masking a hidden fear, but Joshua was intrigued by her innocence and enthusiasm.

He'd found out that her parents had both died of the plague when she was very young, and her uncle, Shaman, had taken her in shortly after. Though she was young and tried hard to please him, he had no compassion for her, feeling she was more of a burden than a gift, and began immediately to treat her poorly. It was much worse when he would visit Kurmish the merchant who would bring exotic wines back from his travels. Shaman would stager back from the merchant's house drunk and beat the innocent and little Hanna.

Daniel E. Wilson

Hanna couldn't recall the details of how her leg and foot became mangled. She did remember Shaman coming home drunk one evening and going into a rage over her spilling something on one of his prized rugs that Kurmish had brought back from a far off land. She remembered him hitting her and her running to the ladder to escape to the roof. After that she could remember no more until she awoke a few days later in her bed in a terrible pain.

The break was obviously bad, and it was taking Hanna some time to heal, but Shaman made her get out of bed and work soon after. It was probably the fact that her bones hadn't had time to heal properly that her leg became almost useless. Whenever she tried to walk, it felt like it wasn't put together at all, and she could only bare a little weight on it. But that didn't stop Shaman from demanding her to work and keep house for him. Nor did her pains and helplessness keep him from whipping her, sometimes across the face, while he was drunk or if she had done something even slightly wrong.

It was for this reason that once Joshua decided to escape from his own wicked master, he had planned to take Hanna with him. Somehow he knew that he needed to do something for her. That somehow her fate would eventually affect his. How could anyone allow such an innocent girl to remain in such a horrible existence?

Joshua would usually leave for the market a few minutes early in order to talk with her and to share his dreams of being free and having his own life and money, and of being a man that others would admire. He'd tell her of how he'd live in a far off area where there was water, trees, and grass more abundantly than she could ever imagine. He would paint the picture of a peaceful life so well that both could see it plainly. He would also tell her of his plans to escape from his wicked master who had stolen him when he was three or four years of age from his older brother's care while they were taking sheep to the market. He no longer remembered the details or even his parents' faces, but he knew he loved his family and was loved by them as well. That was enough to ignite the passions within him to have a life of freedom and to give Hanna the same chance.

Hanna always did her best to show a happy face for Joshua. Often it was hard for her to smile; especially after beatings the night before, but Joshua had a way of making her feel like life wasn't always going to be painful. Hearing him talk of the life he envisioned as a man, a life where he could do as he wanted, wherever and whenever he wanted always made Hanna smile. Nothing brought her greater happiness than hearing the hope pour from Joshua's heart.

So it was that on the morning when Joshua came to the market with the plan to escape later that evening, Hanna was shocked and nearly cried out when she heard his words. Although happy for Joshua, Hanna knew in her heart that any joy she'd had came from him, and the thought of losing that happiness brought fear to her heart and tears to her eyes.

As Joshua read the panic in Hanna's eyes as he told her of his plans, he was more certain than ever that he needed to take her with him, so stepping closer to her, he quietly whispered, "I want you to come with me".

CHAPTER 2

Dangerous Escape

Hanna's heart leapt. The thought of escaping her wicked Uncle, and going on an adventure with Joshua was almost too much to hope for. In her few years, she had seldom left her cruel captivity except to help at times with purchasing food at the nearby market while Shaman slept off a night of wine. Almost instantly though, her fear of being a burden to Joshua shrouded her heart.

Joshua could see that she was torn in her thoughts. He could see her eye fill with both fear and hope, as he searched her scarred olive colored face. Joshua placed his hand on her arm and said he understood if she was afraid. "I am afraid as well, and doubt I can make the journey a safe or comfortable one for you either. But I know that you don't deserve the abuse you receive here at the hands of your uncle, and I'm certain it won't get better."

Hanna's mind whirled, but she couldn't bear the thought of never again seeing the fire of life that shone from the eyes of her young hero. So with fear and excitement bursting inside of her, she decided it was worth the attempt and agreed to go with him.

"Very well then" said Joshua. "I will come an hour before they close the gate to the city. I heard your uncle tell the merchant that he would be meeting him later this afternoon. Apparently the merchant has some business your uncle is very interested in, and I'm certain they will be preoccupied until morning."

Hanna shook her head in agreement, and a cautious smile grew on her face. Joshua had asked her to be a part of her life. She had to go.

While Joshua was in the market Hanna did her daily chores. As the day moved slowly by, she quietly gathered some items for the trip, including those she'd had from her parents that her uncle either hadn't sold or considered useless. Some of these items would be good for the trip, but she was careful not to pack too much knowing that she would have a hard enough time moving through the night with her bad leg. Joshua would likely end up carrying most of her goods as well.

As evening came and her uncle had gone off to the merchant's, Hanna finished her packing, taking some bread, dried fish and meat, and a lamb skin of water. She also took the crude walking crutch that her uncle had given her some time back when he realized that her foot wouldn't heal enough to walk without some aid. His only thought being that she would need it to do her chores and earn her keep.

Joshua was there at the appointed time. The city gates closed three hours after sun set, giving them nearly eight hours of night to travel as far away from the city as possible. They would go east towards the mountains as best they could. It was in the opposite direction of where Cekil dwelt, so few if any would recognize Joshua, and none would recognize Hanna. Hanna was ready with her belongings and food. To her it seemed like a lot, but to Joshua it was little.

"Hurry, Hanna" said Joshua. "I know this will hurt your leg to move quickly, but we need to be as far away from the city as possible. We also need to make it to the gate within the half hour or we may be caught by the night guards."

"I will go as fast as possible, Joshua" said Hanna. "My leg feels strong, and I have been getting better with my crutch, so I won't be a burden."

Luckily, from where Hanna's uncle lived to the East Gate was the narrow part of town. The walk would only take about fifteen minutes for a normal man, but for Hanna, it would be a difficult trek in the needed thirty. With the adrenalin running through their veins and the streets being unusually quiet this particular evening, the two hurried on.

Just as they arrived at the gate, they could hear the guards giving the last call before closing the gate. They only had a few minutes before the guards would be coming down from their towers along the gate to push it closed and lock it for the evening. If this happened, the two would have to ask permission to exit, leaving a trail for Shaman and Cekil to follow. Joshua thought it best for them to sneak through the gate while the guards were climbing down from the watches, so they had made it there just in time.

Josh and Hanna just arrived at the corner of the nearest home when they heard the call. Hanna was out of breath because of the fast paced walk with her crutch, and both were shaking nervously. She knew this may be her only chance ever to escape the cruelty of her uncle's home, so she was ready when Joshua pulled on her sleeve and told her to hurry.

As they slid alongside of the gate, they could hear the guards coming down their ladders. As usual, they were heavier men who weren't in the best of condition. Usually the city hired men who were no good at other labors and were selfish and cruel to keep the gates. It was a long and tiresome job that was tedious at best, but most men who would take such a job normally didn't have a family to go home to and usually didn't care about anyone else's worries but their own.

Realizing that one of the guards had made it to the ground just as they neared the gate caused Joshua and Hanna to freeze in fear. They could hear the big man leave the ladder and start his walk towards them as they cowered in the shadows. But as fate would have it, while the other guard was just finishing the climb down the ladder, he missed a rung near the bottom and fell with a huge "whumph" as he hit the ground.

The first guard was nearly on top of the children, who were hiding along side of a wagon next to the gate listening. But hearing the sound of his clumsy comrade's body hitting the ground, he turned his lantern away from the children back to the ladder, and with a shrill laugh went to aid his fallen companion. In an instant, two shadows hurried through the gate and moments later heard the gate being closed, and the sound of freedom being locked into place by the unsuspecting guards.

Joshua finally broke the silence and gravity of the situation when he said "Whew. I thought for sure we were caught back there. That would have been a bad way to start off one's escape, eh?"

Hanna started to giggle with Joshua's comment. More out of pent up relief and nervousness than because of the humor of the moment. Then she became solemn and said, "I hope no one else saw us on our way. Although I'm terribly frightened of running away, I'm more frightened of going back to Uncle Shaman and bearing the brunt of his wrath."

"You don't need to worry about that any more, Hanna" said Joshua. "We'll be far away from here in a few days, and you'll never have to see him again. And I'll make sure no one ever harms you again either. From now on, you can consider me as your personal Moses, delivering you from your slavery to that wicked man! For now though, we will have to move quickly to get as far away from the city as possible. I have been down this road a few times with my master, and we should be able to reach a small cave I know of by morning's light. Can you walk until then?"

"Yes, I'm certain I can", said Hanna. "As excited as I am right now, I could walk for days!"

CHAPTER 3

Evil From the Well

It had now been three years since they'd escaped the city, Shaman, and Cekil. It wasn't easy to start anew, but Joshua had learned much in his few years, and Hanna was always encouraging. Joshua never ceased to be amazed that Hanna could keep her hopeful attitude alive, even when things were tough and food was short. Though scarred and maimed on the outside from the abuse of her Uncle Shaman, Hanna's spirit seemed unscarred on the inside.

As Joshua was reliving their escape and the adventures they'd had since, it was no wonder that he didn't notice the two dark figures lurking just the other side of the well. And with the darkness of the moonless night, he would have had difficulty seeing even the gleam of the blades that each of the shadows held.

As he neared the well, Joshua heard a slight rumble in the bushes that took him out of his thoughts. "Who's there?" he asked with a start in his voice.

"Just a couple of travelers", said the voice of one of the dark figures. And within an instant, the two were within arms reach of Joshua.

"Now, what would you be doing young master, out alone on a night such as this", said the gruff voice of the second figure. "Doesn't seem the smartest thing to travel alone in these parts at such an hour"? The man reached out a hand and grabbed Joshua's tunic and flashed the blade of a knife towards him. "As a matter of fact, seems like anyone who'd be out on a night such as this would have someone to be hiding from".

Joshua's mind raced. Chances are he could outrun these two, but he would need to leave his water pots and carrying sash behind, and he couldn't afford to lose these if he didn't need to. And since he didn't have anything of value with him, he was confident that the two men would let him go once they found it so.

"I've been busy during the day." said Joshua in a gruffer than usual tone with a slight slang. "And who needs to have folks watchin' what ya do anyway?"

It was nearly the middle of the night when he arrived, and Joshua knew that few were out so late. He had heard stories of certain bandits on the Shiloh highway, but he hadn't heard of any instances being near Malik.   Of course, these two could have been gathering some water for themselves and thought they'd take advantage of the moment as well.

"So let's have it then. Certainly a hard working young man like you would have some kind of purse on him, eh?" said the first man who seemed to be a little more uneasy with the situation.

Deciding not to run and leave the pots, Joshua thought he'd see if he could convince these two that he had nothing of value, and maybe he could have them leave him alone completely.

"Sorry you've gone through the trouble of getting me this evening". Joshua was using a slight accent of the Samaritans while he said this. "I've not with me except my cloak. But you can check if you'd like". With that Joshua laid down the sash and pots, in case he had to make a run for it, and held open his arms.

"Hey now, so you're from the north, eh?" said the second man, as he grabbed tighter to Joshua's tunic and started feeling around his middle area where most people kept their purse. "And likely on the hide I'd guess", said the man as he searched and shook Joshua slightly to see if he could hear anything jingle,

Joshua, now beginning to feel somewhat bolder said, "Yeah, from the mountains of Kalzrin originally. Didn't much like the life of a shepherd up there with my family though, so thought I'd try it on my own out here. But as you can see, it ain't been so easy."

"Well I can't find nothing for sure" said the second man who was searching Joshua, and had released him slightly. "Nothing", he said with obvious irritation in his voice.

"Hey, Cyrus", said the first man. "Do you think this lad could be of help during our job with the caravan? I mean, he seems to be kinda a kin to us, and we could surely use another hand with the task, especially someone young as he."

"Sounds like a thought" said Cyrus. "But what's the boy's thought on making a few shekels or gold coins in the deal? I'd say we need to take him out of here a pace and see better what manner of boy this is. For all we know, he could be more trouble than he'd be worth". And with that, Cyrus grabbed onto a sleeve of Joshua and started pulling him around the well, while the other man picked up the pots and followed behind.

Joshua was beginning to feel uneasy again. Things weren't going quite as he'd hoped, but he was still alive, he had the pots, and he no longer had to carry them. Still, he was uncertain of where they were taking him, and why.

"So, what's it you gentlemen are offering me then?" Joshua shot out not quite as bold sounding as he'd liked. "If it's worthwhile, you definitely don't need to drag me along. If it's worthwhile?"

"Oh it's worthwhile alright" said the first man. "Definitely worthwhile! At least as long as we run it right."

Joshua had figured that these two were not a part of an Apiru gypsy group but were probably just small time thieves who had wandered into the area. They obviously were not well educated and probably on the road for many years. They definitely didn't smell so good. Not that they smelt of sheep, fish, or some other odor that could qualify them. They just smelled as though it had been some time since they'd bathed.

He hadn't been pulled along far, when the two stopped at what looked like a small abandoned structure. It was hard to tell where they were exactly, or whether the place was actually abandoned or part of some property. It didn't seem like there were any buildings nearby, at least none that Joshua could see.

"Alright, here ya go" said Cyrus. "Get on inside here and let's take a better look at ya". And Joshua was given a little push through a broken door and into the candle lit room.

Cyrus and the other man, named Mahli, came in right after him still holding the pots. Joshua could now see that his two captors were dark men, not much taller than himself, with worn clothes and dirty countenances. Joshua would have guessed that both were in their early thirties, and had obviously come from a hard life of little success.

"Have a seat boy, and let's take a look at you" said Cyrus.

So Joshua sat down on a blanket near the candle that was sitting on a small table made of some rough hewn wood. There was little else in the place, which other than having the walls intact, seemed to have been without use for some time.

"Do ya want some bread or water?" asked Mahli. "Can't offer much more."

Joshua, still studying the two and his surroundings, asked for some water. His mind was on the moment, torn between his escaping and the curiosity of the proposition these two were offering him. It had been hard for Japed and him to make ends meet, caring for their little flock and Hanna as well. Their tents were wearing, and winters were hard, so Joshua thought he should stay and hear what the "job" could be. He'd also felt that his captors weren't out to harm him without a reason. He knew he could easily out run them and that they wouldn't go out in daylight at all.

"Like we said, we're looking at the possibility of making some real money in a couple of days, easily enough for three. But it will take guts and teamwork." said Cyrus. "And you may be a big help in making it work if you've got the courage".

"Yeah, it's a great opportunity!" said Mahli, a little overly excited, as he brought some water in a not so clean wooden cup for Joshua.

"But first, let's hear more about you", said Cyrus.

Joshua had talked to a number of other travelers and shepherds that came along the river over the years and had gotten some general information about many areas. So he knew that the people of the north were thought of as rough vagabonds and felt that he could devise an adequate story and insights that they'd believe him and not look for too much detail. He also felt that the more he pretended to "hide", the more these two would like him.

So, within a few hours, Joshua had given them enough "untrue" details about himself that they were satisfied that he was akin to them in many ways. And indeed, he was as he talked about hiding out and being wary of all. Unfortunately, it wasn't too awkward for Joshua to be in the company of such bandits. He had seen his share of the "takers" in life to not feel out of place.

But, as the night passed, Joshua better understood the intent of the task they'd planned. Apparently a caravan had come from the north and was camped just west of them along the Shiloh to rest and water the animals. Being a lean company, the caravan had relied on local vendors and merchants along the trail, and Cyrus had heard that the masters were of the wealthy type, and likely carrying treasure to Jerusalem. He also heard it would be staying a few more days along the river and had been looking to purchase a slave or hire someone to accompany them for the remainder of the trek. That someone could easily find out where their money and any treasures were, and Joshua fit well into the plan!

CHAPTER 4

A Desperate Loss

Hanna was worried when Joshua didn't come back from the well, but she always worried about him when he went off to the well late at night. The dry season limited the water they could get during the day. She had awoken early and was waiting for Japed to come out of his tent when she saw him coming from around the rocks nearby the sheep pen.

"Good morning, young lady" said Japed. "I knew you'd be up early this morning".

"Have you seen Joshua?" questioned Hanna in a worried tone. "Is he working with the sheep? Is he OK? I had a terrible dream about him that woke me up early."

"No, I've not seen him yet this morning, nor have I seen any signs that he'd returned. I was up early as well and have been caring for the sheep". Japed had a worried look on his face where he tried to keep a smile. "We don't need to worry about Joshua, that's for sure. He's definitely the wisest young man I've ever known".

"Well I am worried" said Hanna. "And I'd like him to come back soon".

Hanna hadn't remembered feeling this nervous in some time. Her normally hopeful and cheery face was actually discolored and unusually out of place. It was the first time she'd felt lost and out of sorts. Normally, she'd have started preparing their breakfast of cheese and bread, but she had not taken thought of this at all.

"Come" said Japed. "Let's grab ourselves something to eat, and afterwards, if Joshua doesn't come back by the time we're done, I'll take a quick walk towards the well to see if I can find him. Heck, knowing him he's probably found someone in need and is even now helping them along."

So the two sat quietly along-side one another, but Hanna had a hard time eating anything. Her stomach was nervous and hands actually shook slightly. She'd never felt like this that she could remember. "Something had to be wrong", she thought. The feeling was somewhat reminiscent of the fear she had of her old master.

"All right, all right. You clean-up and take some of the water and grain to the sheep so we don't have to worry about them, and I'll get myself prepared to head out to find Joshua. And then you'll see that all of your worrying was for naught". Japed tried his best to keep a smile on his face while he said this, but even he was worried for Joshua's safety. Joshua had gone many times on the same mission but had never failed to return back as early as he could, knowing that Hanna would be worried.

Japed had hurried himself along, preparing for the worst. He had taken his staff and cloak, though he really didn't need either of these, and hid a long knife underneath his cloak so that Hanna couldn't see it. He had tried his best to be casual in front of Hanna so she wouldn't worry any more than she needed to, but he was worried more than he would normally have been as well. First, because it was unusual for Joshua to be gone so long; second, because he didn't like leaving Hanna alone with the sheep while he went away as well. Something in his gut was not right with all of this. He had a worry that wouldn't be normal in such a situation.

Japed had been alone for almost 30 years when Joshua and Hanna had come across him tending his few sheep in the mountains just west of the city they had recently escaped from. Joshua didn't tell him much, but looking at him, and especially Hanna, Japed had deduced most of their situation and decided to befriend them for a time until he could figure out more of the situation.

The three had become as close as any family could. With Joshua's quick mind and passion to put all he had into every effort, he quickly became exceptional with caring for the sheep and knowing how to migrate them with the seasons. As they spent the years together caring for the sheep and sharing their dreams, Japed had become a surrogate father to his two young companions. And with Japed getting older in years, his heart to leave a legacy of some kind had made him very cautious for Joshua and Hanna.

As Japed hurried towards the well at Shilo, his mind was racing with thoughts of concern. He'd never before worried like this for anything. He knew Joshua would have returned to the sheep with the water and let Japed and Hanna know if he were going off somewhere else. Something must have happened!

SHEPHERD'S SWORD

As he came close to the well, Japed could see that the local residents were already gathering around it for their morning water rations. None seemed to be in any state of hurry or worry, and coming closer, they greeted him with the typical morning blessing and proceeded to discuss the typical politics and drought, with many comments on the Kings high taxes and the difficulties of making ends meet. But he heard nothing that hinted of an event surrounding Joshua, so Japed casually walked around the well area to see if there were any clues that Joshua had even made it there.

As he was pretending to look at something towards the river, Japed came to the bushes where the thieves had tied up Joshua, and he noticed some unusually broken branches and shuffled dirt. Then, in the thicket, he saw a small piece of torn cloth that he was certain came from the scarf that Hanna had made Joshua.

Japed had been gone for nearly four hours looking for more clues about Joshua's whereabouts, but finding none his worries were redirected to Hanna. With both he and Joshua gone, it was certain that she would be worrying herself to the point of sickness, so he headed back towards their camp with the thought of coming back later that afternoon.

Japed was now more worried than ever! What would he tell Hanna? How could he leave Hanna with the sheep and go in search of Joshua? "Hanna couldn't care for the sheep alone and she definitely couldn't search for Joshua, especially not in this area!" His mind reeled with worry, and the walk seemed to take forever before he finally made it to camp.

Then, with even greater shock, he found that Hanna had closed the sheep into their pen, had given them the last of their water, and was gone!

CHAPTER 5

The Twisted Angle

It was a long night for Joshua as well. The more details he had heard, the more he became uncomfortable with the situation as well as with his captors. It seemed that their plan was both dishonest and dangerous, and it just wasn't in Joshua to take something from another without earning it.

Unfortunately, Cyrus had observed Joshua's uneasiness with their plans as well, and realizing the importance of having this innocent looking youngster as an integral aspect of their arrangements, and in the midst of their discussions, quickly grabbed Joshua and using some strong rope, he and Mahli tied together his hands and feet.

The next day, Joshua awoke early feeling uncomfortable and troubled. His thoughts were on Hanna and Japed and their worry of him. Things hadn't gone as he'd hoped. As intrigued as he was with the thought of a rich caravan coming through the area and the potential of doing business with the owners, he couldn't imagine taking anything that didn't belong to him. Yet the thought of being rich and the ability to give Hanna some much needed medical care for her ever worsening legs did run through his mind.

Joshua worked at the ropes for some time trying to get at least one hand free. He had to be quiet though since his captors were only feet away from him. He felt that if he could get one hand free, then he'd be able to carefully loosen his feet and at least make a run for it, but as he worked at the knot, Cyrus woke and looked straight at him.

"So young one," said Cyrus. "I hope you slept well. You will be having a busy day today if all goes as planned."

"I slept as well as anyone could with his hands tied up, I suppose," said Joshua in his rough voice. Joshua had realized his facial expressions had nearly given him away, and he wanted to again make the two thieves believe in him well enough that they would release him from the bonds. "What's for breakfast?"

Cyrus got a smile on his face with this. "Oh. So you're a demanding gent when you've had your sleep, eh. Well, we'll be having something to eat soon enough, I guess". And with that, Cyrus hit Mahli on the side and said "Get up you lazy old fool!"

"Awe, now what'd ya do that for? It's just barely morning!" Mahli was definitely not a morning person. He'd spent so many years hiding in the dark of night from the authorities that he'd become accustomed to sleeping during the day and being out and about during the night.

"Let's get things moving," barked Cyrus. "I've got a feeling we need to move earlier than we planned, and should take a closer look at the caravan before the morning is too bright."

So the three quickly ate more of the stale bread and old cheese and had some sort of hot liquid that Joshua had never had before. It tasted like bitter bark or something, but it was good for washing down the dry bread and hard cheese. It amazed

Joshua that someone would live a life like this, always running and never having anything, and then realized that he had been doing the same thing, only for different reasons.

Cyrus had decided to scope-out the caravan alone and leave Mahli to watch Joshua. The sun was still new when he left, and he only took along a staff and some other small items, including some charcoal from the fire and a papyrus bark to draw out the caravan layout and capture some notes.

"So", said Joshua. I guess you and Cyrus have been working together for a long time, eh? Seems he has things under control and knows what he wants."

"Yup. Cyrus sure has some smarts." said Mahli. "We've been partners for a long time. Almost as far back as I can remember. And he's always been the same, looking for something big enough that would give'm a rich kinda life."

Joshua thought hard about this, too. He had lived a life very similar to Cyrus and Mahli, but his was one where he planned to earn his success. He was certain that these two had never thought of that. Then he wondered what the end would be of their efforts. It seemed to him that many who worked hard never got ahead, while some who were cruel and selfish did. He remembered the old passage that the sun shined on the just and unjust alike, and it made him upset. "Why would those who were evil have as much success as those who were good?"

As the morning dragged on, Joshua had a chance to take a few short naps between some confusing stories Mahli chattered about. He was still tied-up in the smelly old shack, so comfort wasn't so easy to find, but with his lack of sleep the night before, he found what he could.

His biggest worries were those of Hanna and Japed. He knew that they would be searching for him, and he didn't like the thought of making Hanna worry. He was looking for a way to make an escape throughout the morning, now worrying more about Hanna and Japed than his water pots.

Unfortunately, Cyrus wasn't gone long enough for Joshua to have made a set plan of escape. He came back as excited as a man like him could be, talking wildly about riches beyond anything he'd ever seen and how simple a target the caravan was. While mapping out the camp, he overheard two of the servants discussing their departure that day to the south and Jerusalem.   He had also heard the servants talk of their need for another person to help on the journey, and they would need to find a market soon in order to purchase someone who knew animals.

With this, Cyrus, still believing that Joshua could be a good ally, had laid out a plan that would get Joshua to become an insider. This would allow him access to both information and goods. As his plan unfolded, Joshua became more intrigued with the possibilities than of the hazards or deceitful intent.

"Why not go along with this," thought Joshua to himself. "After all, doesn't the sun shine on the just and unjust alike? Doesn't a man have to look out for himself in this hard world? And if I don't do something, Hanna and Japed will continue to live a life of hardship and struggle, and Hanna may never get the help she needs to fix her legs. Maybe this is Jehovah's way of letting me help her."

Cyrus explained his plan to the two. Joshua would hire on with the caravan, find out where the treasure was held, and in two nights, steal away with what he could, meeting up with the two bandits as they followed the caravan. As Cyrus went through the plan, he watched Joshua's expressions and concluded that the young man was intrigued and anxious to do his part in this scheme.

Finally untying Joshua's legs, the three headed swiftly for the caravan camp.

CHAPTER 6

An Unhappy Reunion

Hanna had waited for Japed to return but was so worried for Joshua that she spent most of her time crying and praying. She had worried about Joshua in the past when he would do some dangerous task or go searching for a better pasture for the sheep, but he had always come back when he was expected. His smiling face saying, "See! You never have to worry about me!"

But this time it was different. Even if he had decided to do another errand, or had found someone that needed help, she knew he would have come back to inform them of his plans before heading out. Her fears for Joshua and the long delay in Japed coming back made her panic. She began to worry that Japed would not come back as well and so planned to follow after him. She knew the sheep would keep in their pen for the day as long as they had some water, so she gave them the remainder of their drinking water, retrieved her crutch, and started out toward Shilo.

Since she had never been to the well, she was uncertain of the exact path to take, but she knew it was just east of them a few miles. And she was confident that she'd run into Japed on the way back, and her heart raced at the thought that he would have with him a smiling Joshua.

So, on she went, slowly but steadily, with a woman's persistence, still crying and praying, worry gripping her heart more with every step. And as fate would have it, Hanna was somehow able to find and remain faithfully on the main trail to the well. Japed on the other hand, in a hurry to return to Hanna as quickly as possible, had taken a critical short cut over a rocky area that would result in their passing by one another less than twenty meters, and changing both of their lives forever.

As Japed returned to camp and hurriedly searched the area for the crippled young ward, Hanna, though slow, had made good progress towards the well and came upon a crossroad. A crossing of not only roads, but of her life's path as well. For coming directly at her was Kurmish, the merchant friend of her wicked uncle, Shaman.

As soon as Hanna had spotted him she tried to get off to the side of the trail and hide herself, but it was too late. Kurmish had heard much ranting from Shaman about his "wicked niece", and though he had only seen her a few times in the past, it wasn't hard to recognize the crippled young girl on the side of the path before him.

So Kurmish pulled his small caravan up short, jumped out, and grabbed Hanna by the arm and looked hard at her scarred face. There was no doubt. This was the girl that had escaped from Shaman, and he would be happy to see her returned. So without a word, Kurmish ordered his men to put her into the wagon and tie her up.

After a quick but thorough search around the camp, Japed determined that Hanna had followed after him to the well. "What a fool", he said to himself, "leaving the child alone for so long".

May Jehovah take away my very life if anything befalls her." So he rushed off back in the direction of Shilo as fast as he could.

Japed was once again just minutes of seeing the whole event between Kurmish and Hanna as he rapidly ran along the path, catching periodic tracks of Hanna's crutch as he ran. His mind was whirling with fear, fear for both Joshua and Hanna, fear that these two, who had become so important to him, could be hurt or in danger, or lost forever.

As his mind ran over his fears, Japed neglected to see the last tracks of Hanna's crutch in the dirt and ran nearly a half mile past the crossing where Kurmish had captured the girl before he realized he no longer saw her tracks. Japed hurriedly turned around and began to look for any signs of the young maid, but by the time he had reached the crossroad, the daylight had waned and long shadows now distorted the ground, making it hard to see what may have happened. Japed was seized with panic and started running in all directions looking for any sign for the direction that Hanna might have taken or what could have happened to her.

Hanna sobbed uncontrollably while Kurmish's small caravan moved down the road towards the evil man she had only recently been able to forget in her dreams. She had a hard time putting all the pieces together. "How could all of this be happening", she thought. "Everything is falling apart. Help me Jehovah! Please help me!"

She cried out for Joshua and begged for Kurmish not to take her back to Shaman.

"Please, please, sir. Please don't take me to my uncle!" Hanna forced out through her sobs. "Please have mercy on me." As Hanna broke down into a torrent of tears, she was unable to think of anything else but her wicked uncle's tormenting smile and the hate she would see in his eyes as he beat her without a touch of human remorse.

Kurmish was a business man. And Shaman, though not a good friend, was an influential man who bought much of the goods the merchant would bring back. "It was only right then to return this girl to him", thought Kurmish, "and maybe it would be profitable for me as well."

But Kurmish also remembered how he felt when he saw the fresh scars on the girl and how he had hurt for her when she was crippled by the abuse. Though he knew that Shaman had the right to do with her as he would, Kurmish never thought it right to treat anyone as badly as Shaman treated Hanna.

Though Hanna's sobs softened his heart to her, Kurmish thought it best not to talk to her or befriend her. She had run away from her master, and the punishment for such could have been death. Remembering Shaman saying that he would kill her if he found her, since she wouldn't bring much on the slave market, made him pity the girl even more.

"Maybe that could be the answer!" He thought to himself. "If I can find someone willing to buy her at the North Jerusalem market and bring back the profits to Shaman, then the girl would not have to go back to such a miserable life, and I will save face with Shaman as well. And for my efforts, it would only be right to take a little profit for myself. It seems the girl has become somewhat independent, even though she still needs a crutch, but I'm certain she would work hard if she knew she would not be going back to her uncle". Kurmish's thoughts solidified as he pondered them, and so he prodded on his little caravan into the setting sun.

As Kurmish and Hanna were carried further down the road, Japed hurried in the opposite direction, seeing some tracks that he had hoped would lead him to a clue, and begging the God of Abraham for mercy and a sign.

CHAPTER 7

Meeting Providence

The feeling of excitement and worry mounted within Joshua as the trio hurried towards the caravan. Within himself he was trying to solidify both the tactics that Cyrus had put together and his thoughts of making this effort a success for his intended end as well. His thoughts of making his escape back to Japed and Hanna as quick and secure as practical, with a few treasures in his pockets.

Nearing the caravan, but still in the shadows of a nearby grove of trees, they could see that it was almost ready to move out. Joshua would have to make quick work of securing service with the caravan if the plan was to succeed at all, so they parted quietly, Cyrus sending on Joshua with some additional instructions and threats as he headed towards the objective, and the two thieves retreating back into the trees.

Joshua approached one of the men readying the camels for their departure, with a friendly "Greetings!"

"Greetings to you as well", said the dark man in a halting tongue who was obviously from another country and a bit shorter and more rough looking than most of those that Joshua had known. "May I help you young master?"

"It is possible my lord", said Joshua in as casual a manner as possible. "I'm a shepherd from the other side of the village there", he said while pointing towards a small village on the other side of the river. "Unfortunately, I've been busy working too much of late to visit your caravan but I am always interested in travelers passing through the area. It has been my hope to someday work my passage on an adventure to another land. Though I enjoy the simple life as a shepherd, I have always been intrigued by travel and adventure."

"So what would your name be my young adventurer?" asked the man with a big smile growing on his hardened features.

"I am Joshua, the son of Jotham", he said with a courteous bow to the man. "But my father has long since passed, and my mother just recently, so you may not have heard the name. Who then would you be, my lord, and are you and your company from a far country?"

"I am Caleb from Ethiopia, servant of Master Melchior who is a very wise and successful merchant and explorer from the land of Persia. It is he who is leading this company on business to Jerusalem." Caleb stood taller as he said this, obviously being proud of his service to Melchior. "I have been in my master's service for many years, and he has taught me many things of this world and beyond."

Joshua was very taken back that a slave would be so proud of his position in life. He thought that all men would yearn and even fight for freedom, as he. "It is an honor then to have had this chance to meet you Caleb of Ethiopia", he said. "Thank you so much for taking a few moments with me, but I can see that you are very busy preparing for your departure. As I had said, I was hoping to find a traveling merchant or explorer in need, but I can see your master has exceptional help already."

"Pray, do not hurry on my young master" said Caleb. "Yes we are preparing to leave as you say, but we are also in dire need of an animal keeper! "I am only caring for the animals at present because we have no other, but to do so, I am neglecting the tasks of serving the master and assisting him with his preparations. But as you can see, we would need someone who can go immediately."

Joshua couldn't keep his smile back. It had played out perfectly, and he knew he was in. "I am both able and willing to come along as your keeper of animals. My partner has said that our profit with the sheep is not enough for two, and I will be leaving nothing behind but my shepherd's staff. Will the task pay enough to allow me to start anew at the destination?"

"Yes, my friend, very well indeed, and you will find no better company than those of this caravan. Come, let me introduce you to Master Melchior before the day goes by us, and we are chastised for not completing our preparations".

With this, Caleb led Joshua to Melchior. He was sitting with another, intently looking over a map and talking about their journey. He hadn't looked up when Caleb and Joshua approached.

"Master Melchior", said Caleb, "I have good news. This young man is Joshua, the son of Jotham from this region, and he is willing to serve as the husband for the animals on our journey. Would that be to your liking my lord?"

"That would be fine, my friend," said Melchior in a polished and polite manner; his eyes looking tired but compassionate. "Please see to him if you will and continue to prepare for our departure. I feel we may be behind schedule and would like to make as much distance today as possible. As I see it, we have nearly six days journey to Jerusalem."

With that, Melchior looked back to his maps, and Joshua followed Caleb back to the animals to prepare for the next adventure. Lurking in a thicket of nearby trees were two sinister shadows, watching and smiling at their good fortune.

CHAPTER 8

Seek, Hide and Find

Japed had looked everywhere for tracks that would give him a clue as to what happened to Hanna, fears and anxiousness gripping him like a death shroud. As the sun began to set, he thought that maybe Joshua had returned, found Hanna along the road, and carried her back to their camp. So he hurried back to their little valley, only to find the camp empty.

Never before had Japed been so unsure and lost. His mind whirled with thoughts of dangers that Hanna and Joshua could have encountered. After caring for the flock with some local grazing, Japed realized that he needed to give them water first thing in the morning. So he decided to take the flock to the Shilo well at sunrise and look again for both Joshua and Hanna, keeping a better eye on the tracks and taking the risk of asking others about his two companions.

Sleep would not come easy to him that night, and as soon as the sky began to brighten, Japed was routing his little flock for the journey. There was a small pen area available for travelers nearby the well that he would rent temporarily as he ventured on looking for his two wards. He would go slowly along the route, always looking for tracks.

Hanna cried herself to sleep that night. Though Kurmish did not mistreat her, he definitely did not show any outward compassion either. Keeping himself aloof and having his servants care for her. They made sure they tied her up so she wouldn't escape in

43

the night. Kurmish was certain that someone would have a need for such a one as her and pay more than the trouble he would go through. He was also certain that Shaman would be happy that she didn't escape without punishment but even happier that he had made a profit on her.

Hanna had dreams of Joshua being lost in a vast desert and calling out for her. Her own voice woke her abruptly from sleep as she cried out his name. It was dark, and the memory of the previous day's events once again brought tears to her eyes. "Why has Jehovah allowed this to happen? What have I done to deserve such a painful life?" She had been so happy with Joshua and Japed, that she finally began to feel that Jehovah actually loved her, as Japed had so often said. Now it all seemed so unreal.

So, with sorrow welling up within her, Hanna fell back into a fitful sleep, cold and alone with her hands tied and an ache in her heart that God was once again disappointed in her and was punishing her for something she didn't even know she had done.

Joshua had helped prepare the caravan with Caleb and had taken great care to work as diligently as possible. He had noticed the quality of everything he saw. Nothing it seemed, was less than magnificent in both make and style, but also that there was a special care in the way things were managed. He noticed that Caleb was patient with the others in the party, but expected everything to be done quickly, quietly, and in order so as not to disturb his master or delay preparations.

So it was that the caravan was quickly readied and began to move towards Jerusalem with Joshua in the rear leading the loaded camels down the path and minding that none had been inappropriately or improperly burdened or tied. He was also watching how the supplies were loaded. He noticed that one of the loads was brought out of Melchior's tent with special care and loaded onto the small wagon.

During the process, Joshua had thought hard on his intended mission. He couldn't help but picture the look on Japed and Hanna's faces when he would return with treasure enough to help them all have a better life together. He also couldn't help but see that both would wonder where he had gotten such a treasure. He knew that Japed would not approve of his taking from others. But he also knew that there was little chance that the two of them would ever be able to make adequate earnings to get the necessary medical care that Hanna needed for her leg with their simple flock. Though she had worked hard to prove herself, he knew the pain was growing with each passing month and felt that almost anything would be worth her being whole.

The day passed quickly as Joshua pondered so many issues. His mind was a whirl with thoughts of both strategy and concern. He knew he had to do something fast in order to get back to Japed and Hanna before they gave up on him, but he also knew that making off with a treasure from the caravan would not be easy.

After the fast day's journey, the caravan stopped for the night. Caleb had given Joshua simple guidance on how to tend to the animals and then went to manage the overall nightly preparations for the rest of the company and his master. Caleb noticed how quickly and carefully Joshua had executed his tasks and was obviously very appreciative that Joshua had joined the company.

"Joshua, son of Jotham, it seems that the heavens have seen our purpose worthy and sent us a great help in you". Caleb's eyes shone their approval as he said this. "It would have been a long day for me had you not ventured into our camp this morning."

"Thank you for your kind words, sir", said Joshua. "I'm certain that you would have done just as well without me".

"No", said Caleb. "There have been many things I've had to neglect while caring for the animals. It was a great misfortune for us when our herdsman became ill and had to remain at a village along the way. Since then, I've not been able to properly tend to my master as I should, and it has weighed heavily on my mind. But now that you are here, I feel that all will be well."

Joshua's mind reeled with these words from Caleb. Not only had he not planned to stay with the caravan, but he had planned to steal from it as well! He had never been appreciated as much as this from another and to hear such praise from a man of this importance was very disconcerting.

After all of the animals had been cared for and other tasks accomplished that Caleb had given Joshua, he lay down in a comfortable bed that was provided him by Caleb. His mind was completely overcome with thoughts of Hanna, Japed, Caleb, and, of course, the two thieves that he knew were following the caravan, having seen them here and there as the party moved along.

Caleb had mentioned that his master Melchior was on his way to Antonia to see the king, and would be rendezvousing with some others somewhere around Antonia. It was a matter of great importance to him, and they had been travelling nearly two months so far to get to this meeting.

At hearing all of this, Joshua was somewhat puzzled. He had heard some very bad things about this king they were planning to see and couldn't imagine that anyone who seemed to be so honest and even noble would desire to travel so far to meet with such a one. He had mentioned something along those lines to Caleb, but Caleb just said it was not his affair to know why his master did the things he did. "I have been with my master now for many years, and he has never been wrong in any matters of true importance that I can recall." That was all he said.

So, as Joshua lay there trying to put the pieces of his heart in order, he realized that he could not dishonor these noble people, and especially not Caleb, by his befriending and then betraying them. In the back of his mind, he was hoping that the caravan was one of general trade similar to those he had encountered with his old master Cekil, where all were selfish and greedy. These men were definitely different, and he knew he had to explain himself to Caleb in the morning and ask his forgiveness. Though he could steal away in the night without detection by either Caleb or the two thieves, he could not allow himself to do so, and with this, he fell asleep with thoughts of Hanna and Japed filling his dreams.

CHAPTER 9

Captor and Free

Hanna had eaten little during the trek, her heart saddened beyond anything she had ever felt before. Each mile was wrought with worry for Joshua, Japed, and herself. She did notice that they weren't going in the direction of her old master's city but didn't think much on it. She no longer had hope for herself or anything, giving way to bitterness towards the God of her ancestors for giving her hope and then smashing it to pieces.

Japed had made it to the well without finding any other tracks that would indicate anything of either Joshua or Hanna's whereabouts, except for the end of tracks that Hanna's crutches had made. But an early morning light drizzle had even made those hard to see any more, in addition to the added traffic and trampled mud in areas around the crossroads where Hanna was captured.

Japed had asked those at the well and in the area about seeing either a young man or young crippled girl, describing Joshua and Hanna, but none had seen anyone of their description or even heard of anything amiss in the area. After spending nearly two days seeking clues or tracks on either, Japed finally gave up his search in the area, paid for the care of his sheep and use of the pen, and took his flock back to the little ravine, thinking it best to wait where the three last saw each other.

The next morning for Joshua was fast paced. He felt it best to get the animals ready as quickly and properly as he could in order to show Caleb that he was not a typical thief. He also had nervous energy that demanded action.

As the caravan made its way towards the days intended objective, Joshua put his thoughts in order for telling his story to Caleb. He realized that Caleb would bring the issue up to his master and that Melchior could have turned him over to local authorities or demand his services until he reached Jerusalem. But Joshua knew he had to tell Caleb sooner than later.

As the caravan stopped for the mid-day meal and care for the animals, Joshua had asked Caleb for a chance to talk. So the two sat somewhat apart of the company and Joshua, with embarrassment and shame, explained the situation with as much detail as he could in the short time to Caleb.

"I know this is all too complicated to give you full account, and I fully understand your disappointed and anger", said Joshua, "but I have now been gone from Japed and Hanna for over three days, and I am certain they are more than a little worried about me".

"You are correct", Caleb said with his face towards the ground as he moved some dirt around with a twig he had been holding. "I am disappointed indeed. I'm disappointed that you had lied to me, tried to deceive me in order to take that which wasn't yours, but mostly that I find myself without your help over the remainder of the journey.

"I do thank you though for your honesty in this and," Caleb paused slightly to ensure his words were deliberate and understood, "if you have a true commitment to this young lady and partner of yours, then you should follow through with this commitment to them first. Unfortunately, I believe you have lost more than just a few days but an opportunity as well. I still need help and would have paid you well if you had stayed on with us."

They had discussed the situation for a few more minutes and later during the remainder of the day. Caleb suggested that Joshua work through the day to pay-off the deception he had planned and to allow him the opportunity of the evening to make an escape from the two shadows that had been following, who Caleb said he would take care of later. Caleb also gave some additional insights into his master's plans for their journey and had suggested that if Joshua had made it back to Japed and Hanna and found that they didn't need him for support, that he would talk with Melchior about hiring him back on if he so chose. He said that they would probably be in Jerusalem for a few days, and he could catch up to them if he found it possible to do so.

So it was, as the trek of the company came to the night's place of stay, Joshua had thought hard about all he had heard and what his plans would be for his journey back to Japed and Hanna. He hated the idea of coming back empty handed after leaving Japed to do all the work with the sheep over the past few days but knew Caleb was correct in his suggestions. Joshua's heart raced as he thought about seeing Hanna. He knew she would have been worried about him, and he hated the thought of her worrying or causing her any pain. He was more than excited about seeing her beautiful smile, deformed though it was.

Joshua had been given a few provisions from Caleb to take with him, along with a warning that he tell none of what he knew about the caravan and their mission. Though Joshua had only known Caleb for a few days, he felt closer to him than any he had known besides Hanna and Japed. He had silently prayed that he would somehow meet up with this genuine man again sometime in the future. So, as Joshua collected his goods for his journey, he couldn't help but clasp Caleb's hand with both of his own, thanking him for his understanding and help, wishing him health and success in his journey.

The night was colder than usual, but Joshua walked as a man possessed towards what he hoped would be a happy reunion with Japed and Hanna. He knew he could walk faster alone than the caravan had gone but that it would still take nearly a full day of straight walking to make it to them.

CHAPTER 10

Sold !

Time dragged on for Hanna. She allowed the hurt and bitterness to grow in her heart. Even her captor, Kurmish, had noticed that she was more solemn than he thought normal, though her solemn attitude made it easy to deal with her. She ate little and talked even less, and what little shine her eyes had held, had been slowly dulling.

The wheels that carried her quickly from Joshua were like a wrench turning her heart into knots. Even as they rounded the hills southeast of Ramallah, with the glitter of Jerusalem in the distance, Hanna felt no excitement. She was certain that at every turn, she would meet her cruel uncle and be tortured for her escape a few years earlier.

As they neared to the city, more people were rushing by the company. Though most were from the local area, nearly as many appeared to be foreigners with merchandise and goods piled high on their beasts or carts. She noticed that all seemed uneasy, and she took comfort in their being unhappy as well. Few carried smiles on their faces, and none seemed to even acknowledge Kurmish or his small company.

Readying themselves for the evening, Kurmish was talking to the man who probably owned the small area they were staying at. It seemed that Kurmish had been here before and had intended to stay for a few days. It seemed too, that they weren't the only travelers that had merchandise they intended to sell, but Hanna also noticed that the merchandise of the others included slaves.

After talking to the man, Kurmish returned to Hanna and told her to eat something. "It is not good that you are not eating", he said in a kinder tone than she had before heard him speak to her in. "Tomorrow I will take you to the market to sell. Though I cannot allow you to go free, I also cannot allow you to go back to your uncle, so we will chance your fate on the market, and see if you will be bought by another who will assuredly treat you better than Shaman."

This news did indeed give Hanna some hope. She didn't like the thought of being sold to another whom she didn't know, but there could be nothing worse than going back to her uncle. So Hanna ate, and her night's sleep was more comfortable than any since the crossing. Kurmish didn't want her to look too awful in the morning in order to get as much as he could in the market.

The next day was dreary and threatened to rain. It was probably not the best day for an auction, but Kurmish had Hanna and some of the other goods he'd brought along readied. After an early breakfast, they left for the city.

Hanna wondered about Joshua and Japed. She had left off hoping for any good, and tears began to form in her eyes as the realization of her being sold to another could take her even further from the two men she loved, and make it nearly impossible to return. Her feelings that Jehovah wanted to punish her for some unknown reason continued to grow in her quickly hardening heart.

The market was busier than any place she had been before. The little town she had grown up in was nothing compared to the northern outskirts of Jerusalem. People were rushing everywhere, and anything you could imagine was being sold. Everyone seemed to talk fast, and many were trying to sell their wares or offer their services to those who had passed by. In the center of the commotion was the place she had dreaded, the slave auction platform.

Hanna had decided that she would do her best to not look crippled and show a strong front in order to ensure her purchase by someone who wanted her for more than a menial slave. She felt that if she had value, someone who had a need would be more likely to buy her, but more importantly, she didn't want to be passed up and go back with Kurmish to her uncle.

So it was that as the morning drew on, slaves were being bought and sold like pigs. Hanna had noticed that many of the slaves were from different lands, darker than those of her country, and some even black. She knew that many had been beaten, and all had the look of torment or death in their eyes. She hated the thought that she was just another one of these "belongings" being sold and that her value was determined by what she could do, not who she was. "What an unjust world," she thought.

It was Hanna's turn to go to the platform with another slave that Kurmish had taken along. He had been one of those that had been accompanying the small caravan and helping out, but Hanna didn't know he was a slave to be sold. He was a smaller, older man who had mostly helped Kurmish with the animals. Not much of a man left, but he was quiet and caring. Kurmish would try to sell them both together in hopes that jointly they would have a greater chance of being sold.

As the auction for them began, a number of men had come up to them to look over the merchandise. Hanna was furious at the way they were treated and handled by these men, though most hadn't seemed to be interested. As a matter of fact, most of those who had been bidding before didn't seem to pay these two misfits much attention at all. Obviously they weren't worth much.

Kurmish had been telling of the attributes of the two slaves while Hanna and the other were being "appraised ". Hanna had heard little of his selling pitch but had taken notice when he started to ask for bids. He had started out at a lower price for the two than she had heard from any previous bidding, and this humiliated her as well. "I am worth as much as any other," she thought to herself. "How dare they judge me by my looks". She could feel her face reddening as Kurmish received more laughs than offers, and his incredibly low request wasn't raised much by the time he started to ask for final offers. "I hate these people," said Hanna under her breath.

Hanna was looking at the other man being sold next to her, and she could see he, too, was embarrassed by his value in this life. It was the first time she'd even thought about him. "Where had he come from? Was he taken from a loving wife and family?"

As she thought of this, she was startled to hear the Kurmish saying, "Sold to the gentleman in the back".

She and the man with her were then herded down the stairs and towards a well dressed shorter dark man in the back of the crowd. The man didn't say anything to Kurmish but handed him what looked like more money than she thought the bidding to have been for, and stealing a look at Kurmish, saw a look of satisfaction on his face as he took the money and turned to leave without acknowledging either of the slaves he had just sold.

A feeling of relief came over Hanna that she would not be sent back to her uncle, but immediately following that came a feeling of fear. "What manner of man do I now belong to, and where are we to go," she thought.

She looked slowly up at the man who had just purchased her from certain torment, trying not to seem too proud. She felt that if she had looked overly confident, the man may beat her for her pride. But nothing of the kind had happened. As a matter of fact, the man looked down at her with a look of compassion. He then did something she never expected. He cut the bonds that held both her and the man that was sold with her and motioned them both to follow him.

CHAPTER 11

A Sad Reunion

Though he didn't have any sleep the ·day before, Joshua walked towards the north as fast as he could. At first he was worried that Cyrus and Mahli would have noticed that he had escaped the camp and come after him. Then, as the hours went by, his fears were more on his long absence from Japed and Hanna.

It was a challenging journey for Joshua. Every step he took closer to Japed and Hanna seemed to make him worry more about the two he had grown to care about so much. He didn't know why he had these feeling of foreboding, but they grew in his heart with each step.

Joshua had only slept a few hours in the darkest of the night, before he started up his journey again. He was certain that as long as he was on the right path, he'd make it back to the ravine before the sun set. He had minded their route towards Jerusalem to ensure he knew the right road and trails to take. He'd also found that Caleb had packed him some food for the journey along with a little water skin. His heart went out for his abandoned friend but knew he was doing the right thing. He was also certain that Caleb would find a replacement for him at the next city.

So it was that as the sun was setting, Joshua found himself walking through the familiar rocks and over the lightly worn trail that lead into their small camp. Joshua was so excited he almost ran the last mile.

"Japed, Hanna", cried Joshua as he came around the last bend. "Hello!"

Japed couldn't believe his ears and nearly jumped out of his skin at Joshua's voice. "Over here, Joshua", he said with an excited and almost trembling voice. "Over here with the sheep!"

Joshua came running up to Japed with a huge smile on this face and grabbed the man he had so many worries about. "Japed, it is so good to see you, my friend".

"It is so good to see you too my boy", said Japed. Then his eyes dimmed with the realization that Hanna was gone, and he would need to tell Joshua.

"What is the matter, my old friend", asked Joshua, though he was still smiling. "Were you that worried about me that it has hurt your heart? Surely you could care for the sheep without me for a few days?"

"Joshua. Though my heart is glad to see you and I have great joy at your return, I have sad news. While I went to the well in search of you, Hanna followed after me and has vanished. Though I have searched for her these last days, I have found nothing of her whereabouts."

"What is that you say? How could that be?" Joshua was now sobered by the thought of this young, defenseless girl being lost and alone. "Is what you say true?"

"It is, my son. When you had not returned from the well, I had gone in search of you and left Hanna to care for the sheep. I thought I would find you and bring you back before evening, but after finding no clue of your whereabouts, I returned to find her gone. She apparently had worried more about you than was sensible and tried to follow me to Shilo. I had followed her tracks to a crossroad where they disappeared and believe she was either found hurt along side of the road and cared for by someone coming by or taken by someone who would have had other ideas for her".

At hearing this, Joshua allowed terrible thoughts to run through his mind. His thoughts raced with the possibilities and his stomach felt like he had been hit. He knew he had to find her at all costs.

"Japed", said Joshua. "I am so sorry for my delay in returning and feel that if anything bad happens to Hanna, it will be my fault. I must look for her first thing in the morning. Will you go with me?"

"Of course I will", said Japed. "We can talk of what has happened this evening and prepare the sheep early in the morning for an immediate start. We have enough money to care for the sheep for a month of travels if we need to, but hopefully we will find her soon and in good health.

The two talked of their days until late into the night. Joshua shared everything with Japed and asked for his forgiveness for permitting greed to enter his heart.

As they both made very poor attempts at sleep that night, Joshua had allowed his mind to run over a few of the things

Caleb had told him. Caleb had seemed to have more faith in the God of Joshua's ancestors than any one he had ever met. As Joshua lay there looking at the stars, he wondered how a God who supposedly had made all there was, the great "I AM", could allow so many evils to be in the world. He especially wondered how He could allow Hanna to go through so much pain and now be taken from him and his care.

As Joshua wondered on these things, his lack of sleep and worries over the past few days caught up with him, and he slept through the star lit night until awakened by Japed early in the morning.

"We must move quickly," said Japed. "I fear that we may have more rain coming soon, and we should get to the crossroads to look at what is left of the tracks before it comes."

So the two hurried through their morning preparations as fast as they could, eating little, and started their herd off in the direction of the crossroads. They didn't talk much and both carried a worried countenance as they moved down the trail.

"Here is where Hanna's tracks end," said Japed. "Notice that you can still see a few of her crutch marks here to the side of the road. It almost looks like she hadn't left this spot since I can see no other tracks that she would have made in any direction."

"I agree with your thoughts," said Joshua with a tired sound in his voice after searching the area for additional clues. "I can't make anything out of the tracks, except that these wheel tracks there seem to have stopped and shifted around a bit right here".

Joshua pointed to some tracks about a meter from Hanna's last crutch mark and walked through the scenario as if he'd seen it happen. "It seems the cart had stopped here and possibly that someone had jumped from the cart there" he said pointing to a few heavy footprints along side of the path. "It also seems the cart and its company went along this road here, south".

Japed was embarrassed by Joshua's findings. "I must admit that I was in such a rush to find Hanna that I hadn't noticed this. I chased some tracks north before giving up and going back to camp. I believe you are correct, and we should follow these tracks south immediately.

The sun had risen well above the trees as the two set off after the tracks. Their minds filled with worries for their journey and concern that they would need to be mindful of the sheep. Both knew that going would be slow compared to someone who is moving down the road in a cart, and each prayed silently for Hanna's safety and that their efforts to find her would be rewarded soon.

They had seen an unusual amount of traffic on the roads for this time of year, which added to the difficulties of keeping the flock of sheep in order and moving in the right direction. This coupled with their attempt to follow the tracks of the cart they believed to be holding Hanna had made going very, very slow indeed.

Thankfully, though there had been many travelers over the road during the previous days, the cart that they followed had a unique pattern. A piece of the right wheel had apparently been knocked out, so the pattern in the tracks made following them somewhat simple. The two men grew in confidence that they were at least on the right path as they stopped for the night.

As the two had followed the tracks, and it became apparent the cart was going to Jerusalem. Japed had mentioned that a large market was held in northern Jerusalem this time of year, where almost every imaginable item of merchandise could be found. "When I was younger, I would bring my sheep here for the sale, but I had disliked the place and the price I could get. It's a hard place and I always worried that my sheep would be stolen and I wouldn't be able to do anything about it."

"I don't care much for the idea that Hanna would be taken to a place like that", said Joshua. "What benefit would someone find in her that they would carry her along with them there, I wonder?"

At this Japed's eyes shadowed over. "The market is also known for its success in selling people. It is the largest market in Jerusalem for slaves!"

At this Joshua had a terrible sinking feeling in his stomach and looked hard at Japed. "Let's pray then that we are not too late in finding her, if we find her at all?" Joshua held back a gasp as he thought of Hanna being sold into another cruel life and he not being able to find and rescue her. But he wasn't going to let doubt take hold of him. He would spend the rest of his life if he had to, looking for her.

CHAPTER 12

Beauty in Ashes

Hanna had been ushered along by her new owner, along with her slave companion, who she had heard say his name was Kamal.

It seemed that Kamal and the new master were from the same country, or at least knew the same language. As the three moved through the crowd towards their destination, the master and Kamal talked as though they had known each other for years. Kamal even shared a smile with his new master here and there and seemed to be almost happy.

Getting away from the crowd, the three were able to move easier. Kamal relaxed his hold on Hanna's arm he had held to help her move along through the crowd but now felt it best for her to walk at her own pace with the crutch she held onto. Kurmish had taken her crutch just before they came to the market and gave her a small staff to use so Hanna would appear less crippled than she was.

The new master seemed to be a very pleasant man, though he talked little to her except to keep her moving through the people. He did go slow enough so she wouldn't stumble. He even helped her along when they came to a rocky rise.

They had gone nearly have a mile from the market, when they rounded a cliff and came to a camp near a grassy area. Hanna had never seen such trappings of any travelers. The colors and quality were magnificent, and she wondered about the kind of people her new master belonged to. Hanna had noticed that though it was a nice camp, there were fewer people with the company than there were animals.

"Come with me. I am unsure of your usefulness to our purpose, but I am certain you will be better cared for with us than you would have been with the other that was bidding on your ownership". Her new master said this more as a matter of fact than as a way to make her thankful or worried.

Hanna followed along with Kamal and her new master towards a beautiful and finely sewn tent that was alone on the other side of the camp. Next to the tent was a small table and sitting at the table was a distinguished looking older man, grey of beard and warn of face. He was intently looking at some writings he had neatly before him on the table and seemed startled when the three neared.

"Hello, my friend" said the older man, not getting up from his seat. "I see you were successful in your search for help."

"Yes, my lord, and I hope my choice will prove a better decision than my last." As the man said this he respectfully brought Kamal forward before the sitting man. "This is a man from my own village. His name is Kamal, and he was well known as a good shepherd and man of honor, and though he would seem beyond what most would consider useful, I am confident that he will serve you well and prove himself a worthy servant in our quest."

The man then moved slightly aside so that Hanna could be seen by the sitting man as well, but he did not pull her forward as he had Kamal. "And this young one was a necessary part of the purchase. She cost no more, and as you can see, she has not been treated well and may need some time to know her worth and usefulness. She is slightly crippled as well, but she seems strong enough to walk at the pace we go. With our own herbs running low, I am also hoping she knows some local seasonings that would help make some proper food for the journey."

Hanna felt embarrassed as she was being "presented" to the sitting man. Not so much because of the words spoken of her, but because she felt even more unworthy than usual being in the presence of such people. She could feel her face beginning to flush and legs shaking slightly as she stood there, but determined not to show fear. Hanna stood as straight as she could and looked straight at the sitting man, not worrying about her scarred face. She had made a firm decision to never show weakness or anything that would be less than her best.

After introductions to the sitting man, the two were taken to the other side of the camp where Kamal was put right to work with the animals. Her new master gave Kamal little direction but put an appreciative hand on Kamal's shoulder and seemed very glad to have him with them. "We have hurried here to meet with others who will be joining us either later today or tomorrow. I will then be accompanying the master to Jerusalem on some business he has with the king the day after tomorrow, so we need the animals well fed and rested. I feel that the God of this land has sent you to us at just the right time. He surely knows I have needed your services."

The new master led Hanna towards the fire and food area. "The morning has passed quickly, and the master will be hungry as I'm certain you and Kamal are as well. I hope you know how to make up some stew from the food stuffs provided here and can do it quickly. If there is anything that you see missing, let me know, and if time permits, I will go back to the market later to gather it." And with that, her new master turned and walked back across the camp.

Hanna was left to the task of making the daily meal. She was happy that Joshua and Japed had given her the opportunity to test various meals on them, though her experiences had nowhere near as many useful herbs and salts. As she looked over the supplies near the fire, she found many she had known of when she cooked for her evil uncle. "It will be nice to have some of these again", thought Hanna, as she quickly began to add ingredients into the pot of already boiling water.

Hanna had obviously done a good job on the meal. She had seen her new master give her a look of satisfaction, and all had eaten well. She was certain, then, that she would have a chance to earn her own way with her new people. As she was serving, her mind continuously went back to Joshua and Japed and how much she missed them. It seemed to her that she would never see either of them again, and though the meal was pleasant, her heart was heavy, and her eyes were often moist with tears as she prepared and served it.

Just before sunset, there was a commotion in the camp. Apparently, the guests they had been waiting for had arrived, and their arrival was a significant occasion.

The night was a blur. For Hanna, it was spent brewing tea, serving biscuits and special spread, and making certain that the needs of the guests and those of her new studious master, whom she had heard one of the guests greeting him as "my Prince", were taken care of.

"So that is why there are so many wonderful things here", thought Hanna. "He is a prince from another country that is come to do business with the king of Israel!" But Hanna was puzzled. She couldn't even imagine that anyone who seemed as kind as these would ever do business with the cruel king of Israel.

Japed had once told Joshua and her how he had at one time owned a magnificent parcel of land and had many sheep and cattle, and even servants to help care for his possessions. He had been known as a successful man in his region and was prepared to ask a neighboring land owner for the hand of his daughter. But one day, the governor and a hoard of his soldiers came with a letter signed by the king saying Japed had not paid his taxes and that his property and all he owned would be immediately seized.

Japed's face would grow dark, and his eyes would flash with anger as he talked of his cruel fate and the evil king. Had he not escaped while the governor was looking over his "new possession", he would likely have been imprisoned as well.

Although those of the area new of his innocence, Japed left behind the woman he had hoped to marry and was forced to live a life of hiding and struggle as a shepherd in another region.

Joshua and Japed had pushed themselves and the sheep hard on the trail of the cart that they believed held Hanna. Judging by the times it turned off the road to camp, they knew that the caravan they followed was definitely moving faster than they were able to travel with the flock. The carts unusual pattern with the right wheel did prove simple to follow though and gave the two men hope. But what gave the two trackers more hope was that where the fleeting caravan seemed to stop, they could periodically see what appeared to be the tiny imprint of a lone crutch.

CHAPTER 13

A Face to Remember

That evening brought Yom Shabbat and a good time for the two to stop. They had talked little on the trail of Hanna, keeping their eyes and ears alert to anything that would give them a clue. Taking a day to rest and discuss their options was much needed though Joshua would have preferred to continue on.

"I don't see how we can catch up to her at this pace, Japed", Joshua said as they prepared camp for the setting of the sun and the beginning of Yom Shabbat, their day of rest. "I don't like taking a full day of not following the trail and not be able to move on tomorrow evening as well. We will lose two full days in following her".

"Yes," said Japed as calmly as he could. "I understand your concern, my son. I, too, am not fully ready for a stop, but I fear more our displeasing Jehovah. It may be good for us to take a day and seek His blessing on our efforts".

"How is it that you speak as though the god of our ancestors is real and actually cares for our cause?" Joshua's haste in the statement and anger in his voice startled even him. "After all that has happened to you, losing all you had and hoped to have, and being forced to live as a wanderer all these years. And what about Hanna? If Jehovah was real, how could He allow her to lose her parents, be brutally treated by her uncle, and then when we finally begin to have hope, He allows her to be taken from us?"

"Yes, yes I know. It is a hard thing to believe that anyone great would allow such things to happen. I can't even tell you why I hold on to belief after all I've seen. The wicked seem to prosper and those who are good, like Hanna, have to suffer". Japed hung his head as he said this, but raising it slowly and looking into Joshua's eyes he said, "Yes, it would seem that if anything, those who look out for their own good and are willing to hurt others to care for themselves seem to triumph. But I have also seen that just as Moses was forced to flee from Pharaoh and Elijah from Jezebel, in the end, Jehovah does honor those who do justly and punishes those who do wickedly. And it is my hope that in this case, that Hanna will be honored for her pure and hopeful heart."

"Well then", said Joshua. "You pray, and I will do something of value by going to the village in the morning to get some water for the sheep. And I will see if there is any news that will help us find Hanna."

It was a tough night for Joshua. After eating some hard bread and cheese, he lay down near the sheep and tried to sleep. He knew he needed to rest, but sleep was hard in coming. Japed's words of a god who turned wrong into right kept coming back into his mind.

"How could anyone believe such stuff," he thought. "I haven't seen anything of value in this whole land. Everyone looks to their needs and cares nothing of others. If it weren't for Hanna and Japed, I would not think there was anything good at all. Look at the king and all the evils the Romans have brought to this land. How could anyone believe that we are the people of the true God when He would allow such evils as this to control our people?"

His mind worked for hours trying to sort it all out, but Joshua had too many questions that were unanswered by what he had seen and had heard. His mind also raced at the thought of Hanna being hurt again by someone without a cause, or of her being sold to someone who would use her up and discard her when she couldn't do what she needed to because of her lameness. So with such thoughts as these, it was early morning when Joshua finally fell into a fitful sleep with harsh dreams.

The morning came too soon for the two travelers. It was agreed that Joshua would go to the nearby village while Japed cared for the sheep. There were things the two would need in order to continue their pursuit of the tracks, and Joshua was too anxious to sit in the camp.

"Please remember that this is the Shabbat", Japed called to Joshua as he walked to the edge of the small grassy area they had found for the sheep just off the trail. "People will be more friendly than usual because of the day, but they will be wary as well. It seems that there are many things happening these days, and with our being closer to Jerusalem I'm certain they are worried about spies and thieves. Be patient and do more listening than talking. Be careful of your questions."

With that, Joshua left for the small village that was about an hour's walk back up the trail. The day had gone by slowly for Japed. The memory of Joshua's last time away was still fresh in his mind, and he spent more time in prayer for Joshua than he did in the ritual prayers and thanksgiving customary of Shabbat that he had grown up with. He thought and prayed hard for Hanna as well. He pleaded to Jehovah that she would be safe and comforted. He knew she'd still be worrying more about Joshua than herself, and prayed that somehow, somehow, she was safe and hopeful.

Soon he saw Joshua returning from the village a few hours after the sun had seen its peak, and Japed nearly jumped out of his clothes as he rushed to greet the boy. His relief overflowed into hugs and pats on the boy's back. Joshua was almost embarrassed but realized what even this short separation must have meant to this gentle man, and he was humbled by how important he had become to Japed.

"I have been sorely worried about you, my young friend" said Japed as he held the boy's arms and looked at him with relief in his eyes. "Please forgive me for my lack of faith".

Joshua couldn't help a big smile that came across his face as he looked at the man. "Come on now, you worrisome mother hen, how could you possibly think I would not come back as quickly as possible when I had such a short time to annoy you today? I came back after being kidnapped and having the chance to live life like a king, did I not?"

Truly these two had become best friends. Though Japed had seen more than twice the life that Joshua had, there was a bond of friendship and respect that few could say they had ever earned in this life.

"So, come have some water and bread with me and tell me of your day's adventure". Japed still gripped Joshua's arm and over excitedly lead him to a nearby tree to sit.

As they sat for a few hours, Joshua gave as many details of his findings as possible. It was quiet as Japed had suggested it would be, but there was still some stirring in the village. It seemed that along with a large bazaar that was normally held this time of year in northern Jerusalem, there were many others travelling in the area in various directions based on some order by the king having to do with taxes and such. He couldn't put it all together, and most of what he heard was from some of the travelers to the area that had various dialects of speech.

Joshua said he was certain that the cart they had been following would be going to the large market less than a days travel south of them. By the marks being left from the cart, it seemed as though it was heavily laden and moving slow. He also mentioned that he had heard that the bazaar was very popular for selling slaves.

"As I remember as well", Japed said with a worried look. Did you hear of anything specific that would have given clues of the cart we follow or Hanna?"

"Not specifically", said Joshua with a puzzled look on his face. "It seems there have been so many people coming and going through the area that few would have noticed anything unless they had specifically had some dealings with them. I did hear of a merchant who was a common dealer at the market that had come through a few days ago and had stopped for a short visit to water his animals. They had said the man came from somewhere north of the Ayalim Valley towards Ramla."

"Isn't that near the town you and Hanna had escaped from?" asked Japed with a start in his voice.

"Yes. Mevo Modi'im is definitely on the way to Ramla." Joshua got a worried look on his face as he said this, which he knew he couldn't hide from Japed. "And unfortunately, I remember that the terrible merchant Kurmish who was a friend of Hanna's Uncle Shaman had often bragged of his goods coming from 'Jerusalem and the east' in order to get a higher price for his merchandise. If that were so, then he may very well have traveled this route from the east to Jerusalem".

It was a very somber moment as the two talked about the possibilities and chances of Kurmish finding Hanna on the road. It would have been easy for him to spot her with her crippled feet and facial scars left by her uncle.

As they talked, they both became more anxious than ever about moving on as early as they could in the morning towards the market. They knew it would be another two days journey at best for them and their sheep. Their hopes being that they would find Hanna before whoever had taken her had finished his business and moved on.

Early the next morning before the sky had lightened the east, Joshua and Japed had already cared for the sheep and began their trek towards Jerusalem and the market. It was a cooler than average morning for being late in the month of Av, so the morning walk was pleasant, and the sheep were easy to move down the road. Joshua and Japed had no problem following the unique track the cart had left, and so it was easy to discuss various strategies for finding Hanna once they came towards the market. They agreed that they would trade some of the sheep for Hanna, if she was being sold as a slave and they were in time to bid. They felt he would do better selling the sheep than Hanna in the market.

It wasn't long after the mid-day rest that Joshua had grabbed Japed's arm, and with a very anxious look, pointed ahead to a small group of travelers coming their way. A couple of men were walking along side of another well dressed man perched on a medium sized wagon being pulled by two donkeys that would match the type that the two shepherds were following. And it wasn't hard for Joshua to recognize the man as Kurmish the merchant.

CHAPTER 14

Peace and Disquiet

The next few days were a whirlwind of activity for Hanna as she kept the fire going, made meals for the caravan, and cared for other light chores that she had been given. Her new masters and their visitor had seemed engrossed in many discussions and exciting thoughts, and the energy carried through the camp to all. Hanna had overheard a few conversations where she understood a few words and knew that they were on an important quest to see the king.

She was still unsure why such men of apparent graciousness would want to visit the wicked king of Israel and be excited about it. It just didn't make sense. But, on her third day of being with the camp since her purchase, Hanna was told to prepare some food for a journey that her new masters would be taking later that day. So Hanna put together some dried meat, cheeses, various breads, and vegetables that had been cured and strung together. Apparently the masters wouldn't be gone long but would be taking a number of their camels and sheep as well as various packages and goods that seemed to be gifts for the king. She had Kamal help her with loading up the food stuffs she had prepared for the journey and waited to see what she would do next. She also looked forward to a few days of quiet since she hadn't had any since Joshua had gone away.

There were still a number of servants and others who remained behind, including Kamal, so Hanna was kept busy caring for their needs while the others were gone.   It was indeed quieter in the camp as those left behind spent much of their time checking and mending things that had been neglected during their journey. Unfortunately for Hanna, this time of quiet only allowed her more opportunity to think about Joshua and Japed.

Oh how she missed Joshua's smile and the sound of his voice. She would often find herself day dreaming about him and their times together in the field with the sheep or their discussions about life as they sat by the fire. She found her eyes tearing up more often than not at the thought that she may never see this man again and how fate had played a cruel trick on her just when she was finally feeling at ease with her new life.

Kamal would often check on her during the day and could easily see her sorrow. "What is the matter with you, girl", he asked. "Don't you know that this is the best a slave could ever ask for? It is as if God Himself has given us a view of heaven on this earth."

"How can you say that?" Hanna asked him with honest curiosity. "Don't you long to be free?   Don't you miss your family and home?"

Kamal looked softly at Hanna for a moment, and with a distant look in his eyes said slowly, "Yes, yes. I do miss my home. It has been a long time since I was captured and made a slave. Yes, such a long time that I have even forgotten what my beautiful wife and two sons look like. I have been through so many years of bad times as a slave that I didn't think I could live another day, and yet here I am, in the company of great men who believe in a new time and hope for the world. I am happier than I have been in many, many years."

"Well I don't like being just another possession. I had been free for three years before that evil Kurmish found me on the road, and I don't believe any slave is happier than a free person."

Kamal saw that Hanna was very upset while she said this and shook his head slightly in agreement.

"Yes", Kamal said. "I agree with what you say in some ways, but as I have come to know the God of this land, I have also come to believe there is a greater plan to life than what we can see. And I believe that our being sold into this company is another part to the path of our life that will lead us to our destiny."

"I wish I could agree with you, Kamal, but as you can see, I haven't seen much good in this world. Each time I allow myself to hope and dream, another hurt is soon to follow." Hanna's grief with the thought that she would never again see Joshua filled her eyes with tears as she said this, and she turned from Kamal back to her work.

Japed had caught Joshua's thought immediately. The company coming towards them would match the one they were following.

"That is Kurmish", said Joshua in a quiet tone. "I am certain of it".

The two weren't going to have much time before they reached the oncoming company and knew they needed a plan quickly.

"Joshua", said Japed in a hasty voice. "Do you think this Kurmish will recognize you?"

"I am uncertain," said Joshua. "It has been a number of years now, and with my growth and maturity, I am unsure. Though he didn't know me well, he did see me often at the market before our escape."

"Well, we can't trust it to chance that he won't. I will get him to stop and give us some information, and you stay apart with the sheep so that he doesn't recognize you."

With this, Japed moved ahead of their little group so that he would come in contact with Kurmish first. Joshua had walked along side of the sheep and moved them off the path slightly, which would have been a common thing to do.

"Hail, my friend!" Japed had lifted his hand in greeting as he said this and moved just slightly in front of the approaching caravan. "Are you coming from the market?"

The company had come to a halt just before them. Joshua had maneuvered the sheep around to a small grove of trees and a light grassy area but kept within earshot of the assembly. He wanted to hear everything, especially anything that would give a hint about Hanna.

"What can we do for you, sir?" Kurmish was obviously irritated in the disruption.

"My apologies for this interruption, my lord", said Japed with a bow. "Would you happen to be coming from the Shudfa market?"

"Of course we are. Who else would be traveling along this dirty road on such a hot day? What is it you need?"

"Again, my apologies my lord, for the delay. I have never been to the market before, and my master has sent me there to trade these sheep for some goods and a slave girl to help with the household chores. I fear that this useless young helper has made us go too slow to make it to the market in time." Japed kept his eyes facing downward as he talked so that he wouldn't reveal his feelings for this man.

"Well you have not missed the market. It will go on for a number of days yet, but you should have come sooner if you are looking for a slave girl. The best trade days are earlier, but I'm certain that you will still be able to find one. Had I known so many were looking for a girl, I would have increased the price on the one I had sold". Kurmish was feeling pompous and allowed himself to talk more than he should have.

"Oh, my lord, I only wish I had met you on your way to the market then" said Japed. "Since I have not before traded there and am unsure of the worth of these small sheep compared to a slave, I fear I may not do my master well in this venture."

"Yes. Good fortune was not on your side with this. But as pitiful as these little sheep are, the girl I had to sell was even more so. Thankfully good fortune was with me, and I received much more than the whelp was worth. Now move out of my way so we can move on." Again, Kurmish allowed his good fortune to free his lips more than he should, but Japed and Joshua were elated at his boastful frankness.

"Yes, my lord. Please forgive my folly." Japed knew he could not risk taking the whip from Kurmish if he annoyed him too much, but also knew he needed more information about the slave girl Kurmish had mentioned and maybe something of her purchasers.

Lowering his head slightly more, but not moving, Japed continued on. "With my uncertainty of the value of a slave, and what I might expect from these sheep, I apologize for trying to gain wisdom at your expense. Please forgive your servant."

Kurmish now saw a business opportunity and wasn't hesitant in taking it. "It is obvious that your master has sent a wise servant to do his tasks, and I admire your intent. But I too, am a business man and must be on to my next engagement. Your interruption is costing me."

"I certainly understand, my lord. Please don't let me turn you from your task, though I would gladly pay for your time and wisdom." With that, Japed reached under his sash for his money bag, brought out a silver shekel, and held it out to Kurmish.

"Very wise, very wise indeed! I will not disgrace your offer and provide you with some quick guidance into this market, though your pay is insignificant in comparisons to my delays." With that,

Kurmish reached down to take the token from Japed and carried on in a matter of fact tone.

"This market is a very unusual one in that many come from far lands, and you cannot know for certain who you are dealing with. There are great opportunities there, but you must be in the right position to find them. As mentioned, the slave girl that I had sold would not have sold for much on her own. I had to combine her with another slave who was particularly good with animals."

Japed couldn't believe that Kurmish was being so free with information. He knew that Kurmish's arrogance was now talking, and he felt he needed to target the information. "Please forgive me this one more time, my lord. You said that you sold the pair of slaves. Could it be that the one who bought them may not have wanted the girl? Are girl slaves as costly as men?"

"It all depends on the slave and the need", replied Kurmish. If you are not looking for anything of beauty, then you will likely find a good deal. But many come with problems. The one I had traded was lame and likely very useless. You may even find her back on the block when you arrive."

When Joshua heard that the girl was lame, he unfortunately became overly attentive, and moved slightly towards the wagon. And Kurmish now took notice of him.

"Do I know you?" Kurmish asked Joshua. "You look familiar but I'm not sure exactly how."

Japed jumped in immediately. "I do not think so, my lord! He is a stupid boy that has spent all of his years in service of the master, and this is his first time away from the master's house. He is both deaf and dumb".

Kurmish looked hard at Joshua for a few moments, but Joshua put his head down and acted as though he didn't hear their conversation. Kurmish waived it off and pressed to make the discussions end and return to his journey.

"Anyway, yes, you would do best to sell your sheep at the north end of the market where many of the wealthy foreigners do their trade, and then go to the south end to find your slave girl. Maybe you'll find some rich buyer like I had to purchase your sheep. Some of the dark easterners are wealthy and don't know much about value. But enough, I must be moving on."

With this, Kurmish jostled himself in his seat and gave the reins a shake to move on. Japed kept his head low and moved to the side and out of the way of the moving cart.

"Did you hear that? I'm certain that the girl was Hanna, though for a stupid deaf boy I guess I shouldn't have heard anything". Joshua had a playful scowl on his face, but his eyes glistened with excitement.

"I am sorry, my boy. I had to say something to keep you from opening your mouth and giving him more reason to recognize you." Japed's smile and expression revealing the first hope Joshua had seen in him since he'd left for the well.

Joshua had to smile, too. Hanna was just ahead of them, and they now had hope!

CHAPTER 15

A Bazaar Coincidence

Their journey to the market went quickly. Joshua and Japed had pushed the sheep as fast as they could in order to make it to the north end of the bazaar before the sun set the next day. They followed the tracks of Kurmish's cart for some time, but as they neared the Shudfa, travelers were many and the trail hard to see.

"With at least three days passing since Kurmish would have sold Hanna, I am certain we will find clues to her whereabouts outside of the market more so than within. Since those that purchased her and the man slave were looking for an animal husband, it's my guess that they were a larger traveling group that may not have been here specifically for the market." Japed's words were meant to be hopeful to Joshua, but his tone was filled with worry on the enormity of the task of finding her amidst so many. "It may be best that you remain with the sheep outside of the area, and I will do the initial searching. We can move the sheep each day to a new location, and we will search for clues in each new area."

The two talked a lot about the comments Kurmish had made and tried to piece together the parts into a better idea of what could have happened. As they discussed the possibilities, they each felt more uncomfortable for Hanna knowing she would be scared and lonely.

After some time, they found a good spot for their little flock of sheep, and immediately began looking around the area and talking to other shepherds and herdsmen that had taken up a similar temporary residence.

In her camp, Hanna had allowed her frustrations to build while the party was away. She didn't talk to Kamal nearly as much as she should have. She didn't want to hear of his positive attitude and wanted to sulk by herself. She missed Joshua so much, and during the day and while alone at night would find herself tearing up at the thought of him. So her bitterness drove her to work with full vengeance.

"Why would God do this to me"? She would continually ask herself. "We were doing so well, and Japed was teaching Joshua so much. Why, God? Why did You cause this to happen? Am I but a wretch that deserves to be tormented? Have I done something evil against You like the children in the days of Moses?"

Answers did not come, but she pressed on with the hope that she could somehow escape and make her way back to Joshua and Japed. She worried that Joshua may have never come back, or that if he had, the two may have given up on her and moved on to another area. She was unsure of her ability to make the journey back to Shiloh with her bad legs and that an escape from her new masters would be difficult considering how easy it would be to identify her. So she continued to torment herself until her masters and the party returned from the visit to Antonia, the king's palace.

She was then distracted by the definite excitement in the air when they returned. The two sages had been joined by another from their country on the way to the king, and it seemed all had been well received at the palace. Apparently, the king was excited to have the visitors and to share some wisdom of the current affairs of Persia and the world beyond Israel.

Hanna had a hard time understanding the conversations that she could hear, but was very interested to find her masters were graciously received at the palace. As the evening came on, she stayed near the fire cooking, cleaning, and keeping tea water boiling. And though discussions were being held around the camp, Hanna found herself staring into the fire; the flames taunting her with glimpses of Joshua's smiling face.

So it was that the evening passed quickly, and one by one the company melted into the comfort of their quarters for a thoughtful sleep. With the others retired, Hanna sat alone before the fire growing more sorrowful with each dancing flame, until the master came along side of her, suggesting that she retire as well.

The next morning Hanna was told that the company would be going further south, and that she would need to prepare food for the journey.

There were many conversations within the camp as they broke down but mostly a sense of remorse that they were on the move again. It seemed that many had hoped the journey would end with the visit to the king and that they would be returning home. Apparently the masters, whom Hanna now understood to be prophets or priests from Midia, felt that they needed to continue on with their search for the "fire", or something like that.

All was made ready, and the caravan moved on. They were going to go wide around Jerusalem to avoid the large numbers of people, but would not hurry. Hanna was allowed to ride with the food cart along with the master who had purchased her at the market. Though the day was beautiful and the ride in the cart mostly comfortable, Hanna's hopes of retuning to Joshua sank more with each step of the mule, anger mounting towards the God of her ancestors who had given her such a lonely and painful life.

Still a distance away, Joshua and Japed spent the night caring for the sheep after the long and hard journey. The find of a quiet glen with a small creek running along side of it was a joy they didn't expect. With so many travelers in the area, they were certain that a dirty camp would be their lot. Though it cost them four silver shekels paid in advance to stay for two nights, they felt it well worth the price for clean water and light grazing.

Apparently the land owners were on a journey themselves, and a neighbor was renting the land out for them to those "worthy of its use". He didn't like the foreigners and made it plain that he only rented to descendants of Jacob.

Once the sheep were cared for and the small camp prepared, Japed suggested that he do a quick look around the area. The sun was just falling below the trees, and he knew he had an hour or so before it would be too dark to see much.

As Japed started off with staff in hand, Joshua lit a small fire and began cooking some of the last of their meat. His mind was going over the details and information they had received from Kurmish and other details he heard from those they met on the area.

Though Joshua knew he may never find Hanna, he would not allow himself to think on that. He forced himself to see the joy on her face when she'd see him turning the corner and seeing each other face to face. That was one thing about Hanna that he never tired of. When he'd return from caring for the sheep or some other errand, Hanna always had a huge smile of welcome for him. He wasn't sure why he cared so much about making her happy, but it was the most important thing in his life. It hurt him to think that she may be once again in an environment of pain, torture, or loneliness. He knew he'd do anything to see her free and happy again.

It wasn't long before Japed returned from his scouting trip around the area. He had come up from the south along the creek and was carrying a small bag of goods with him.

"Back so soon?" asked Joshua. "I was certain you'd wander around the area for most of the night, considering all of the happenings and many travelers for so close for you to bother".

"Ho and I see you've been relaxing yourself instead of making a grand meal for your wandering friend". Japed once again had a smile on his face. He was happy of their good fortune in travels and finding such a great spot for the sheep. He had also purchased some additional meat, bread, and cheese for their journey and did so at a reasonable price.

"Well it's not much that's for sure, but it's all you left me with while you were out on your relaxing walk through the countryside." Joshua waved Japed over to have some of the stew he had made up and some bread. There were some tubers and wild onions along the creek bank that he found which added both flavor and additional substance to the meager stew he had made during Japed's absence. They'd eaten little on their journey so far, so this was like a feast to the two weary travelers. "So, what did you find on your quest?" asked Joshua.

"We have definitely been blessed in our journey", said Japed with excitement in his voice. "It seems that this is a well traveled road for those coming from the north and east to the market. Though I didn't find anyone with news specific to Kurmish or Hanna, I did find that there have been a number of wealthy caravans that had come through the area asking questions about the market and the events that are happening in all Israel. One in particular had asked about the slave blocks."

Joshua's heart jumped at hearing this. He knew that few caravans would come through looking for slaves. Usually it was a merchant who would purchase a slave and then take the slave directly to a wealthy land owner for a specific purpose. Seldom would the needy master do his own slave purchase.

"This is good", said Joshua. "I am certain that you had found some vital information in that. Did you find out where the caravan was from or where they were going to?"

"Unfortunately the owner of the small market said it was four or five days prior that he had seen the company and had little time for questions. He was certain though that they were Medes or from somewhere in Persia and mentioned that their caravan and animals belied a wealthy host though traveling light." Japed knew Joshua was getting excited with the news so was talking in a matter of fact tone.

"Yes, yes. That's all good information", said Joshua. "But did he say anything that would have given a clue of where they were going?"

"Well now", said Japed. "What was more interesting is that the foreign visitor had asked about travel problems going to Antonia. The same place I believe your caravan at Shiloh had intended to go".

CHAPTER 16

From Dreams to Reality

Hanna had become more depressed with each mile traveled. Even her new master was somber as they drove on. He had hoped to be going back home and had periodically talked to Hanna of his wife, children, and the beautiful gardens of the master's land. Only Kamal seemed excited, coming along side at times to share a smile with the two riders and offer a word of hope and excitement. Gestures which though kind in nature strengthened the grip of Hanna's internal struggles.

"What are these crazy people doing", Hanna wondered. "Why are they continuing on when they have already met the king and given him their gifts? Why would Jehovah take me further away from Joshua and Japed?" In her heart she was hoping that the caravan would turn back north, towards Shiloh.

It was a hard day's ride mentally, and Hanna looked forward to the stop that evening. They had gone most of the way around the southeastern side of Jerusalem and were now in a quieter area along the north Kidron River. There were still many people traveling the roads. She particularly noticed the number of sheep herders, which of course made her long for Joshua even more.

The night's meal was good to all the travelers. Hanna's time at the camp while the masters were at the palace was well spent in pre-arranging meals that were simple to make but with all of the herbs, made them exceptional for the continued journey. The men of the caravan were very happy to stop, eat, and get a good night's rest. It was told to them that they would be leaving early in the morning once again and should keep things as packed as possible in preparation.

The masters of the caravan had spent much time going over various documents and maps and spent the evening discussing routes and timing. They seemed to be most interested in comparing charts with the stars, which Hanna had seen routinely, and took it as some part of their religious belief or their way to ensure they had good luck in their travels.

As the evening wore on and quietness settled over the caravan, Hanna's loneliness returned, and she began to think of ways that would allow her to escape and return to Joshua. She now feared that each new day was going to take her further from him. She would even accept beatings if she were caught in hopes of a chance to succeed in her escape and in finding Joshua and Japed.

With these thoughts Hanna fell into a fitful sleep, dreaming of Joshua and her walking hand in hand beside him along a peaceful and beautiful stream. Her heart and her body, dancing with joy along side of "her" Joshua, pulling him with her to see a cascading waterfall, or their reflections in a pool. And as she looked at herself, she would see a beautiful and unscarred face, smiling alongside her handsome Joshua.

Her dream was so real, so inviting. She could see Joshua's strong and caring eyes looking deep into her soul and felt his approval and love. But, as she stared into the pool, noticing his youthful face and perfect lips, hideous scars began to form around her own face, causing her to hurriedly pull away in shame. She quickly looked at Joshua to see if he had seen the scars as well, but nothing in his eyes showed he had seen anything less than beauty. And as they looked at each other, she felt Joshua's strong arm wrap carefully around her small waist and pull her close to him. She could feel his breath against her face, and the nervousness welling in her stomach, as though her whole being would melt into a pool of happiness.

But before she could receive the kiss she so longed for, she was startled awake by a subconscious knowledge of a forbidden love and the realization that her dreams were but mocking her reality. The tragedies that life had handed her were inescapable.

Elsewhere, sleep did not come quickly for Joshua and Japed either, but when they fell asleep, they did indeed sleep well. Japed was certain that Jehovah was smiling down on them and routinely mentioned that to Joshua. Joshua, on the other hand, spent the evening strategizing.

"Could it be that Hanna has been sold to the very same caravan that I too was company with?" Joshua's mind was a whirl with the thought. "How could this possibly be? There are so many travelers these days, and this market is huge. Could it have even been Caleb who purchased Hanna?"

Joshua shared everything he could think of specific to the caravan, and the two went over every detail and thought. If it were Caleb's caravan that had indeed purchased Hanna from Kurmish, they both felt it would bode well for them. If it had been some other caravan, and they chased after Caleb, they could lose valuable days and clues. It would be best to follow hard after every clue of this eastern caravan, but at the same time, seek for more definitive assurance of this possibility.

The next morning, the two were up early, and began their planning immediately.

"At the speed with which the caravan could travel, they would have arrived in this area about three days ago", said Joshua. "I don't believe they would have tarried around the market area for long, considering the typical person that would be in the area. If the masters of the caravan had traveled here to see the king, they would have settled on the other side of the market closer to Jerusalem."

"I believe you are correct", said Japed. "I believe there is a river just east of Jerusalem that would be quieter and give a short day's ride to the palace. If Hanna has been sold to this company, it may very well be that they would be in that area."

It was decided again that Japed would search the area for additional clues and go to the market, while Joshua would tend to the sheep.

"While I am gone, maybe you could sell that one smaller sheep that seems to be having a hard time with the journey. We could use the additional money as well as a swifter herd." Japed thought more on keeping Joshua busy than the sale of the sheep.

So Japed took up his staff and started towards the market while the morning was still young. He told Joshua he'd be back well before the evening meal and to have something ready for him, teasing Joshua about the "so-so" meal of the previous night.

With Japed gone, Joshua cared for the animals and positioned them closer to the road so he could market the small sheep that Japed had mentioned. Joshua knew that they were low on funds, but also knew that he could get a fair price for the little lamb. They had taken good care of the flock, and they all had a beautiful white fleece.

So, as the day dragged on, Joshua pondered the words of Japed from the night before. It did seem coincidental that they could be following the same caravan that he had chanced upon after being kidnapped by the two thieves. "What would be the odds of something like that happening", he thought to himself.

He pondered the thought of a god who actually cared for mankind, and though he was Judean by birth, he had little interaction with the synagogue or any religious activities. The only religious acts he knew of would be the blessings one merchant would give to another after trying to take advantage of each other.

Now Japed would weave stories of Abraham, Isaac, Moses, and David into many of his talks by the fires at night, but they all seemed too unreal. Why a god who supposedly created all things could have intentionally created a world with so many problems was beyond his comprehension. "Why would he allow men to be so selfish and uncaring? And then why would he constantly have to send prophets along to 'fix' what shouldn't have been so messed-up in the first place?" It just didn't make any sense to Joshua.

As the day went on, Joshua pondered these thoughts, and became more uneasy with his own life. Maybe he wasn't much different than most that had turned from this "God". This was a god who seemed to give men freedom to do what they wanted, but sent plagues or enemy armies against them when they turned away from him and pursued their own pleasures or other gods.

Just after the sun had reached its peak, Joshua felt it was time to water the flock. An area farmer came by who was on his way to the market to purchase a lamb. He was happy to purchase the small one Joshua was to sell at the price he had hoped for. The farmer didn't like bargaining and hated the market, so he offered a reasonable price right up front that Joshua gladly accepted without debate.

"Now here", thought Joshua. "I could have waited here all day and not sold that lamb. And just as I had given up for the morning, I sell it for the price I needed. How is it that some things work out so well, and other things that are more important, like Hanna being beaten and scarred for life, turn out so wrong?"

Joshua was still pondering the strangeness of life and worrying about Hanna when Japed returned. Joshua had made a good stew with the last of the tubers and onions he had used the night before but also added more herbs he found in the field He also had time to cook up some flat bread from meal Japed purchased the day before, and had cleaned off some of the good cheese they had been saving, since he felt this may be the last night they would be in such a beautiful area for some time.

Japed was famished. Apparently he had not eaten all day and had walked more than any other day in his life.

"So?" asked Joshua. "Were you able to find any valuable news?"

As the two men sat and ate of their meal, Japed shared that he found more information on a caravan that had come through the area that fit the description of the one they were looking for. He said that most of the people were very busy and wouldn't give the time to talk of other things. He did, however, receive enough information to confirm what they had thought earlier. The caravan would likely have gone south of the market to settle if they had planned to visit Antonia. It was the closest reasonable area for such.

"Joshua", said Japed. "I found the slave block in the market. The owner said that a few days before, a man from the north had sold two slaves to a man from the east and was paid handsomely. One of those sold was a disfigured young girl".

Joshua was both elated and angered by the news. "How could anyone treat Hanna like this", he fumed. "Couldn't they tell she'd had enough in life without being treated as an animal?"

The two had talked again until late in the evening, sharing their thoughts and hopes, and strategizing about their actions on the morrow. Japed was certain of the route the caravan would take towards Antonia and that they could narrow the distance if they left early the next morning. The two friends, worn from a long day, finally settled down to an anxious sleep.

CHAPTER 17

To Close for Comfort

The next day was a hard pace for Joshua and Japed. They were glad to have given the sheep some rest, but they themselves were weary. The thought that each day may take them further from Hanna was a continual attack on their minds. But the hope that they were likely on the right path to find her drove them on.

All along the way, the two would greet other travelers and ask them news of the road. Often they were bold in asking about a wealthy caravan, or a cripple young girl, but none said they had seen anyone that matched the description.

It was late in the day with the sun less than two hours from setting when they finally reached their hopeful destination. It was a beautiful area with old trees lining a small flowing stream and grassy patches in many areas. Definitely not the sort of place a shepherd and his flock would be welcome. So the two men took the flock across a shallow area of the creek, allowing them a moment to drink of the clean water and graze quickly, and found a small cleft in the hills just minutes away.

They made a small fire and had a quick meal of some dried bread, dates, and cheese that Japed had purchased the day before. After discussing their plans for the next day, Joshua told Japed he was going to the inn they had passed just before the crossing at the creek.

"Are you sure you want to do this?" asked Japed. "Though this is a beautiful area, I can assure you it's not a safe one. I am certain that some of those we passed on the road would have had evil intentions towards us if they felt we had anything of value. The closer you are to the palace, the more danger you are sure to find."

Joshua answered quickly, "I'm sure of it. Something of importance is there for me to know or hear, and I must go. Maybe 'Jehovah' has given me a vision or is calling me there?" Joshua said this with a hint of mocking in his voice, but in his heart he wondered if this had been the case. He had this intense urgency within him that he needed to go to the inn, and maybe it was the 'small voice', like the one that came to Isaiah on the mountain, that pushed him on.

So Joshua removed his cloak from his carrying sack, and left for the inn with a small amount of money, and a great amount of curiosity.

The inn had both rooms and a tavern for the travelers to the area. It was obviously a very popular establishment with nearly all of the tables full, and the dim candles casting busy shadows around the room. Joshua had never been in an inn before, and the smell of the inhabitants and the heavy air made him long for his open fields and the soft breezes of the country.

Joshua grabbed a chair in the back of the room in a small inconspicuous area where he could see and listen to those at the inn without much notice. He was uneasy in such an environment but knew that most of those in the room had been drinking too much wine and wouldn't pay him much attention.

So Joshua quietly sat himself down and ordered a flute of wine and bread from the middle aged, well nourished lady that apparently owned the establishment, and turned his attention towards the others. "My word", he thought aloud. "You would wonder if any one worked during the day. They seem to be full of energy and very loud".

The innkeeper brought back his wine and a small, still warm plate of bread, and Joshua paid her the half shilling she'd asked for. It seemed like a lot for a drink that didn't taste all that great. But Joshua held it in his hand and sipped it slightly as he watched and listened to the men in the room. As he'd hoped, no one paid him much attention.

It seemed that most at the inn were not from the area. They talked about travels, women, and business. Apparently no topic was sacred in here, and though most carried foreign accents, Joshua was able to understand many of their conversations. He determined that the majority were merchants that had come to do business in Jerusalem, and all were willing to share their stories and boast of their business savvy.

After a long day's trek, Joshua quickly tired of the loud talk and arguments of business, the Romans, and women, and started to feel the need for more direct questioning concerning Hanna. But, as he rose from his chair, the door to the inn opened, and Joshua fell back into his seat as if his legs had been cut out from under him.   There, as a taunting menace, stood the unquestionable profile of Cyrus, the thief.

Joshua, quickly recovering, sat back and brought the cup of wine to his lips in order to conceal his face. The realization that he was trapped in the back of the room with no easy escape sent a chill through his body. Since he had told Caleb of the intentions of Cyrus and Mahli, he was certain that the two were confronted by the company of the caravan and was amazed to see Cyrus free, or even alive.

Joshua did little to bring attention to himself, while Cyrus came in gruffly and ordered a drink from the keeper. Apparently Cyrus was here for a meeting and after receiving his drink, walked over to the table of a man who had been sitting quietly on his own not far from where Joshua sat. Luckily the chair Cyrus had taken faced away from Joshua, allowing him to relax his posture and look more natural.

Though the room was loud in general, Joshua could overhear most of what the two men said, and at first, heard the usual greetings and dialogue.   It was obvious that the two knew each other, but also apparent that they had not seen each other in some time, with both being cautious of the other. As Joshua listened to their dialogue, he was certain their meeting was purely business.

With his back to Joshua, Cyrus was harder to hear than the other man, but since he was naturally louder, Joshua could pick-up most of his words. Apparently they were discussing a "job" that needed to be done quickly and probably needed two or three men to accomplish. It would have a big payout but also have a high amount of risk.

"We can't mess this up", he heard Cyrus say. "I've already lost much on this and am worried that I may have been noticed, though I can't say as they're more secure. They left at dawn heading south and seemed to be in a hurry."

Joshua couldn't hide his interest in Cyrus' words, though he tried to keep his face concealed by looking down at the table. Unfortunately, the man with Cyrus noticed Joshua's interest and was keeping an eye on him throughout their conversation. When Cyrus made this last comment, Joshua couldn't conceal his interest. The man with Cyrus held up his hand in front of Cyrus indicating caution and loosely pointed towards Joshua.

The next few moments were a blur to Joshua. Cyrus carefully looked behind him at Joshua, who had shifted his gaze to the floor and tried to hide behind his wine cup. But his attempt to hide was unsuccessful, and Cyrus recognized him instantly, though he turned back towards his companion with little evidence that he had.

A chill had gone completely through Joshua as Cyrus turned towards him, but he was unsure whether Cyrus had gotten a good enough look to identify him. And he now became extremely uncomfortable with his being in a corner. After waiting for a few moments for an indication of Cyrus recognizing him, Joshua felt he had not, and thought it best to leave the place as quickly as possible. After taking another mouthful of wine, he quietly put the cup down on the table, stood to his feet, and walked to the door using a path that would take him as far from Cyrus as possible.

Unfortunately, as Joshua approached the door, he saw Cyrus quickly rise from his seat and head directly for him, intercepting Joshua as he pulled open the door. He also noticed him reach under his tunic for what he knew would be a knife.

Cyrus helped usher Joshua outside, with a mean grin on his face. "So, lad, what brings you to this area? You must be looking for an opportunity too, eh? Maybe changed your mind and thought you'd come back for some goods from them that you put onto our trail? Ya know, it was a lucky thing that I escaped from the trap you laid for me and Mahli but not so lucky for him. If he's not in jail, I'm sure he's been hung on one of them there Roman trees."

Cyrus was so close to Joshua that he could smell his foul breath and see the evil look in his eye. He also saw that Cyrus had taken the knife fully out of his tunic and was now eager to use it.

Joshua didn't have time to think of what to do, he just reacted. His elbow swung hard at Cyrus' face, hitting him along his left cheek and staggering him back, but Joshua was not quick enough to stop the blade from cutting into his left side and slicing along his left arm. Luckily for Joshua, his youth and strength carried a heavy blow with it, and Cyrus was severely dazed and almost fell backwards.

With that, Joshua turned and ran as fast as he could into the night and away from his attacker. His head reeling with the thoughts of what would happen if Cyrus caught up with him, and the pain he felt in his side. But the adrenalin flowing through his body made him run like a cat, and he put more than enough distance between himself and Cyrus before finally slowing down.

Listening intently for the footsteps of the big man, Joshua tried to catch his breath as quietly as he could, still holding his side. Though the pain was extreme and blood soaked through his cloak along his side and from his arm, he was certain that neither were serious wounds. He was glad he'd acted as quickly as he did, knowing that Cyrus would have killed him right there without hesitation. He'd heard enough from the man to know he had no concern for life, at least not for anyone else's.

Joshua still hurried as he moved along, thinking about what he'd heard from Cyrus and wondering what Japed would say. "So this is what that 'small voice' was telling me to do", he thought to himself. "To get myself killed by a maniac outside of an inn full of worthless people?"

As he stumbled into the camp, Japed could tell immediately that something was wrong. By the light of the small fire they'd started, he saw Joshua holding his side and the blood caking his side and arm.

"What happened to you?" the older man asked in a panicked voice. "Where are you hurt?"

Japed pulled Joshua towards the fire and helped him remove his cloak. It was easy to see the wounds in his side and on his arm, and though the bleeding had stopped, Japed could tell that they were serious enough to worry about, but probably not life threatening.

"This is what I get for my prayers to Jehovah yesterday", Joshua said as his head became light and he limply eased back so Japed could look over the wounds. "I ran into an old friend at the inn, that thief Cyrus, and he wasn't happy with me."

CHAPTER 18

Painfully Close

Japed was obviously concerned for the young man. His hands were shaking as he cleaned the boy's wounds, and his voice showed his anxiety. "Didn't I tell you that this was a dangerous land? You could have been killed!"

"You have certainly said a truth in this, my good friend. Had I known the results, listening to that feeling in my heart would have been the last thing I would have done. It seems that when I do, it only gets me into trouble." Joshua said this with a sudden tiredness as the adrenalin began to ebb and pain took its place.

"I did hear some interesting news, though, from Cyrus himself!" Joshua felt a little pride swell up, and he was almost smug in his statement. "It seems he's been following the caravan of Caleb in order to carry out his plans to rob them of their treasures. And as you can see, he's obviously mad at me because of his lost chance earlier and his partner Mahli being captured."

With this, Joshua finally succumbed to the events and was shrouded in a painful semi-consciousness. Japed carefully continued to clean his wounds with hot water, healing herbs, and salve he'd had for the sheep. He knew these would help Joshua heal and hopefully keep the wound from becoming infected. And though he worried immensely about his young companion, his worries lessened as Joshua's breathing became heavy and consistent and he fell into a much needed deep sleep.

Joshua awoke early in the morning with a terrible thirst. His side felt like a mule had kicked him. The memory of his encounter with Cyrus was almost like a dream, but the pain in his side was very real.

Japed heard Joshua groan in pain as he tried to rise. "So I see you're still alive, my adventurous young friend?"

"I guess I don't feel so good", said Joshua. "I feel a bit cold and shaky, and my side aches. Do we have any water?"

"We do, but you lay still, and I'll bring it to you. I'm sure you have the beginnings of an infection going in your side, and the best way to get over it will be to relax". Japed reached over and touched the boys arm in a reassuring manner, checking for a fever as well.

The morning was well from the point of breaking, and the two took advantage of the time to talk of what happened the night before. Joshua went through all of the details he could remember, but some had been hard to recall. The details of the meeting and words of Cyrus and the man he'd met with were very clear, however, and he was thorough in explaining that aspect.

"So you are saying that this Cyrus man, who had abducted you at the well of Shiloh, has been following the caravan for all these days? He must know there is something of great value there, or he is more vengeful than intelligent. I wonder what it is that possesses him." Japed was truly curious of this man and wondered what his part would be in this unique adventure.

"I don't know", said Joshua, "but the hate and cruelty in his eyes were evidence enough for me that he has no good intent. I'm certain he'll be following the caravan until the time is right for him to execute his plan against their company. And I'm certain it includes an act of revenge."

As the sun rose, so too did Joshua's feeling that they needed to move on after the caravan as soon as possible. But Japed was worried about the boy's wounds and fever.

"I believe it best to rest a day" said Japed. "I'm certain we won't fall too far behind".

"No. We must move on as soon as we can. If the caravan left yesterday as Cyrus said, we must find out where they stayed and the direction they took as soon as possible. We cannot allow them to get too far ahead, especially with our being so close." Joshua was obviously adamant, though he ached with the thought of walking all day.

Japed knew that Joshua would not allow himself to take a day of rest, and though he feared for his young companion's health, he knew that Joshua would only worry himself to misery if they delayed the pursuit. "Very well", he said, "we will go as soon as we are able, but you must promise me that if you become weak, or your side begins to hurt too much, that you will allow us to stop and rest. And since my night's sleep was interrupted by a half crazed young man as well, a long day of travel is certainly not something I plan to do."

The two prepared for a quick departure, with Japed caring for the sheep and Joshua gingerly packing their small belongings. Aside from the complaints about the bitter tea Japed had made Joshua drink, they talked quietly about their day's task and where they would look for the caravan's trail. Each fearing that Hanna may not have even been with the caravan they were following but neither willing to mention it.

Japed looked over the wounds in Joshua's side and arm where the blood had filled the bandages and hardened against his skin. After the painful removal of these, Japed applied new salve and bandaging on both and was pleased to see very little signs of infection or reddening around either of the wounds. Japed was visibly pleased with himself that he had taken time the day before to gather some of the medicinal herbs needed to refresh the ointments they carried for the sheep.

As the two men herded their small flock down the path, Joshua felt nauseous and his side ached with each step. But his worries for Hanna and his thoughts of warning Caleb of Cyrus's plans gave him determination to press on. Eventually the aching and nausea were just a slight annoyance to him.

Just before the sun was at its peak, the small company came upon a nice area that travelers obviously frequented, and the two men agreed to stop for a rest and look for clues. Japed thought it best if Joshua stayed with the sheep in a small shaded area just off the trail while he went about looking for clues. Joshua was relieved to rest for a while.

Joshua's rest was short lived, though, with Japed hurrying back to tell of a caravan that had left the area early that morning that fit the exact description of Caleb's. Worry was in his eyes as he told Joshua that others had joined the company and that there was rumor of their being wealthy but dangerous foreigners who had visited the king and may be on a mission of evil intent.

CHAPTER 19

From Hope to Shadow

Hanna was up earlier than usual. Embarrassed by her dreams of intimacy with Joshua, her heart was racing and kept her from falling back to sleep. She could hear a few others moving around but was certain there was still another hour before the caravan would be awake and begin preparing for the day's journey.

She climbed out from under the makeshift bed she had of soft blankets and ground coverings. Though she hated this camp and all it meant, she had never had it so well. It was a colder night than usual, so the added blankets were a welcome source of comfort.

"I'll make sure the fire is hot and tea is ready for the men when they awake", she said to herself. "Maybe today we'll find what it is these strange men are here looking for, and we'll head back north by way of the road we came down on. When we pass Shiloh, I'll escape and find Joshua and Japed."

Hanna had felt that she shouldn't share much of her life with any of her caravan companions. Though her master and Kamal had treated her very well and often asked her about her past, she thought it best to keep the information close in case she had a chance to escape. That way they would know neither the direction she'd go nor location of her whereabouts.

As she was tending the fire, the masters of the joined caravans were talking quietly in a tent, looking over some documents that they had sprawled out on a small table they carried with them. The candle flickered in the light breeze of the early morning. A couple of times they would come out of the tent together and look to the sky as if validating the weather or their directions, then go back into the tent to converse again. This didn't make much sense to Hanna since even she knew they were going south.

The camp began to stir and come alive, and the prince obviously wanted to hurry the small company along. The master gave Hanna a hearty smile when he saw that she had already prepared the morning tea, flat bread, and dates for the company. He could see she hadn't slept well and looked worn. He wished she would confide in him somewhat, but she just didn't say much other than asking questions of him. He felt sorry for the young lady and the past she must have had, and because of this was unusually patient and caring.

"Thank you, Hanna", he said, with a look of appreciation in his eyes. "The preparations you made with the meal and teas will make the masters happy and allow us an early departure this morning while it's still cool. I am uncertain how long we'll travel, but I believe we should be at our destination sometime shortly after the mid day meal. We may even continue on to the intended camp and forego the meal until we are at our planned stop."

Although Hanna was happy for the praise, she still harbored resentment towards this gentle man for her lack of freedom and for his carrying her further away from her home and those she loved. She did allow a slight smile to cross her face, though the scars made her smile look more of a mockery than true emotion.

Hanna's leg was aching, and she felt generally exhausted as she prepared the food for the company and packed for the journey. She almost looked forward to the cart ride so she could rest a little during their day's trek. The idea that she could ride instead of walk was very comforting.

It had proven to be a beautiful day for traveling. The morning continued to be unseasonably cool for this time of year, and as the day evolved, it warmed to a comfortable temperature with a light breeze. With such conditions, the spirits of most had picked up again, and with no real mishaps with animal or cart, the day had found most of the company in light conversation about home, family, and hopes.

Though Hanna had started the day in a tired and less than encouraged mood, she found herself enjoying both the weather and ride. Her thoughts were on her dream of the night before, walking hand in hand with Joshua along the beautiful creek. She could picture his eyes shining out to her with love and praise, as a man would have for a woman he longed for. But with each jostle of the cart over a rock or rut, she was reminded that instead of being near this man she had grown to love, she was being carried further from him with each turn of the wheels.

For the first time in her life, Hanna actually found herself loathing who she was and wishing she'd been someone else, someone beautiful and healthy. She had grown into a woman, and she was feeling what women felt. She wanted to be wanted not just supported. She couldn't help but think that as a young and handsome man, Joshua would eventually look for a mate, and then she would become an outsider in his life.

Though the ride was comfortable, with these thoughts her heart began to ache more with each step of the mule. She had never been one to complain about life or harbor resentment for anything that had happened to her in the past, but as she thought of Joshua being close to another woman, she began to feel lonely and afraid. The enemy of her heart was filling her with hopelessness.

"Maybe he doesn't even miss me", she thought to herself as hopelessness welled up in her breast. "Why was I even created if my life was to be one of torment and hopelessness? And what can life offer if can't be fully shared? Oh God, why? Why am I here and why does it seem you hate me so?"

For the first time, Hanna's heart and soul wanted answers. She was growing up, and was willing to seek out the truth from the God of her ancestors, pleading to know the purpose of her life.

So the day's journey had passed as quickly as her master had said, and they stopped for the evening in a quiet area just outside of a small but busy town in a hilly countryside. It wasn't the most beautiful area Hanna had seen, but the small trees and grass reminded her of Shiloh. The place they found to rent was not large but had grazing and water for the animals and a view of the city.

Hanna and the rest of the company had set themselves to expect a longer than usual stay. Hanna prepared a quick meal for all from the food stuffs she had readied two days before. The next day would be the second Shabbat with the company, and purchases would need to be made at a nearby market.

Though all seemed well for the small caravan, a shadowy figure followed them as they journeyed along the trail, hiding in a small crag along side of a nearby hill when the caravan came to rest. In its dark heart was greed and revenge.

CHAPTER 20

The Interrogation

With the following day being the Shabbat and realizing their nearness to the caravan, Joshua and Japed hurriedly gathered the sheep and began the trek south after the caravan they heard had left early that morning. The journey was tiring for both and painful for Joshua.

As the sun began to set on the beginning of Shabbat, an aching Joshua and a very tired Japed sat by the warm fire in a small opening between two rocky cliffs some distance south of Jerusalem. Joshua fell to the ground against his an Japed's packs, his side pounding to the unmerciful beat of his tired heart. Though reluctant in allowing Japed to remove the wrap and bandages from around his waist and arm, he was too tired to fight or even argue the case.

"Today's walk did not do your wound well at all", Japed had said with obvious worry on his face. "Not only are you still bleeding, but the area is now red and swollen. Thankfully we and those we are following will both be forced to stop for the day because of the Shabbat. Tomorrow, I will care for the sheep, and you will rest."

The two men talked of their plans for a short time while Japed cleaned Joshua's wounds and reapplied the salve. Japed said a silent prayer for his companion who winced during the painful process, asking Jehovah to honor this noble young man who had been through so much in his short life. Japed had always felt

119

that both Joshua and Hanna were undeserving of the hardships life had dealt them, and as a father to them both, wanted to see them blessed and joyous. But what could vagabonds and shepherds ever receive in life but wandering and hardships?

It didn't take the two long to fall asleep, but neither slept well. Joshua spent the night in sweat, fighting off a fever that was attempting to own his body. He dreamt his old master was kicking him in his side, and yelling at him for being lazy. One kick was so hard it startled him from his sleep, where Joshua realized the pain was real, but not from being kicked. But with the exhaustion greater than the pain, he fell back into another painful dream of running after Hanna through his old town, and her master having a hook in his side trying to hold him back.

Japed's dreams too were painful. He dreamt of Roman soldiers and cruel citizens chasing him through a wasteland, his every turn leading to a stony cliff with no way of escape. Yet, just before dawn, as he was once again trapped against a cliff and unable to escape, this time, as the soldiers and angry mob pressed in on him, he fell to his knees and gave himself over to the mercy and grace of Jehovah, the mighty deliverer. At this, Japed awoke to a beautiful light pink sky and a heart filled with peace at knowing that the "Star of the Morning" truly cared for them and would indeed guide their paths.

Rousing himself up, Japed began the morning care of the small flock of sheep, giving them water he had gathered from a small stream they had passed the day before and a small amount of grain he had kept for the Shabbat.

Joshua awoke with a groan. His clothes were soaked with sweat, but his fever had burnt itself out and he actually felt better than he had over the last few days. His side was sore, but it had not bled through the bandages.

"Well", said Japed when he heard Joshua moving around. "How are you feeling?"

"Let's just say that I am glad this is the Shabbat", Joshua said this with a slight smile on his face. "It's amazing how such a small blade can make it feel like your whole side was kicked in. I see you've been awake for awhile?"

"Not too long. The sheep are cared for, though, and I am actually hungry myself. Are you feeling up for something to eat?"

"I'm starved", said Joshua. "I didn't feel much like eating yesterday, so I guess it caught up with me now. What do we have left?"

"Not much. I hope we find a market nearby to replenish our goods", said Japed, again starting to get that worried look on his face, but realizing the course of his attitude, relaxed his spirit and said it was great that Jehovah had taken care of them so well.

Joshua, too, was more relaxed than he had been for some time. "I must thank you, too. You have been like a servant of God to Hanna and me as well, and we owe you more than we could ever repay. And though I remain cautious of trusting in life's providence, I am certain that we will we will find Hanna and somehow bring her back as well."

Japed and Joshua relaxed and talked of the good things that have happened since their first meeting. They talked of hope and dreams, and how the three of them would work hard and make a new life for themselves. They would always be a family. It was truly a refreshing morning, the first in a long time.

Japed looked over Joshua's wounds and reapplied the salve. Both the wounds were still red and slightly swollen but somehow looked better than they had the day before. Maybe the rest had made the difference.

Later in the morning, Japed suggested he'd look for an area they could move the sheep to graze after the Shabbat was over. It had been a hard trek on the sheep as well and an evening of easy grazing would do them well. He also had in his mind the chance to find clues on the caravan but thought it best not to mention this to his young companion.

So after stern advice to Joshua that he rest until he returned, Japed took his staff and began an easy walk towards the hills just south of their camp. Not only was he to keep his trek short because the Shabbat laws, but he also needed to find a simple, short route for the sheep and Joshua to travel once the evening darkness began to fall.

Japed felt good and took in the beauty of the area. He was amazed that this part of Judea, so near the City of David and Jerusalem, would be so peaceful. There were a number of small creeks that obviously ran through the hills during winter, but at this late season of the summer, most of the beds were dry. Still,

Japed enjoyed the relaxed morning and the thought of finding a quiet place to rest for the night.

Following one of the dry creeks that wound towards a green hill he had seen earlier, Japed prayed for God's mercy with his steps. He prayed he would find both a place for the sheep and something of the caravan. He expected to see few people in the area but was certain there would be other flocks grazing on the hill he was going towards.

Japed had walked less than an hour when he came to a small opening where he could easily see the intended hill before him. The creek bed he followed lead directly to it. Next to the hill he could see a few small groups with their animals grazing at the base of the hill that had obviously found the area a good place to rest on the Shabbat as well.

Thanking Jehovah for His grace in allowing him to find such a place, Japed started towards the grove with the hope to find some information from the travelers. But, as he started up the path, a dark figure came towards him with an almost menacing grimace on his face.

"Hoy there!" he heard the man say. "You look to be a stranger around here"?

Japed was startled how quickly and quietly the man had come upon him. "I am", he heard himself saying. "You surely startled me".

"My apologies, sir" said the man. "I was just wondering why anyone would be wandering through these hills here on the Shabbat. I thought it went against the laws here".

It was obvious that the man was not from Israel and had been travelling hard. As he looked him over, something seemed familiar about him, but he was certain he'd never seen the man before. Then it dawned on him that the man's size, his clothes and the pock marks on his face were familiar. He'd heard Joshua describe a man that looked just like this. It was Cyrus!

CHAPTER 21

A Worried Look

Though her masters didn't celebrate the Shabbat that would begin that evening, they did honor it while in the land of Jehovah. So Hanna was busy preparing meals and doing light cleaning and organizing as soon as the caravan stopped. It was understood that they could be staying in the area for a few days.

"How are you feeling?" asked the master in a concerned tone. "You seem less happy than the day you came to us?"

"I am well", is all Hanna could muster up. She had grown more convinced than ever that they were going farther and farther from the two men she loved, and the pain of never seeing them again weighed heavily on her heart. "I am sorry if I am not doing an acceptable job."

"No, no. On the contrary, you are doing a very good job, and the masters are pleased with your being in our company. It is just that I am worried about you." He was talking as a concerned father would talk with a daughter. "Please let me know if you are sick or if you need anything."

"Thank you", Hanna whispered. Her eyes beginning to well up with tears as she turned away from this kind man back to her chores. She wished she could share her heart, but her fears of men and the evils they could do made her frightened of sharing her hopes and desires.

It was a fast paced evening for the company. The masters of the caravan were busy talking about so many things, arguing about dates, history, and all sorts of things that Hanna couldn't understand. They seemed unusually passionate about "the king", and Hanna couldn't help but be bothered by their interest in such an evil man. They almost seemed overjoyed to be near him!

Hanna had completed her chores before sunset so as to keep with the Shabbat and was sitting just away from the main body of people. She marveled at the beauty of the sky as the stars began to shine, and a quiet breeze rustled through the trees overhead.

Joshua was obviously feeling a bit better and was being impatient as he saw his older friend returning in haste. "Well? Did you find anything?"

"I did", said Japed. "More than I would have hoped for. Not only did I find a good place for the sheep, I believe I may have found the caravan we search for as well."

"You did?" said Joshua with even more impatience in his voice. "And yet you came back without Hanna?"

"Like I said, I may have found them." Japed was happy to see the boy excited over the news but was uncertain of how they were to proceed from here. "I couldn't get close enough to them to make certain. I ran into Cyrus!"

A shudder came over Joshua when he heard the name, and for an instant the ache in his side seemed to worsen. "I see", said Joshua, "Luckily he doesn't know you. But what makes you think it was Cyrus?"

"He was a man such as you described, and seemed to be protecting a small hideaway overlooking the green hills I was looking for. More importantly, as I talked to him there near this hideout in the cliffs, in the valley below I saw a beautiful small caravan that would match the one we seek."

At this, Joshua nearly jumped at his partner. "You saw the caravan, then?"

"Yes, I believe I did", said Japed. "But Cyrus was wary of my actions, and by the way he questioned me, I could tell he thought I may have been a spy from the caravan. Even now I am uncertain as to why he let me go."

"What should we do then?" asked Joshua, more as something to say than in looking for an answer. The sun would be setting soon, ending the Shabbat, and their thought of moving the sheep to better grazing was now a small detail compared to the thought that they were so close to Hanna.

The sun was still setting later in the afternoon, but the stars were brilliant in the evenings. The moon was scarce in recent days, so moving the sheep through the hills on such a moonless night would be difficult.

As the two talked of their course of action for the night, they prepared the sheep for the trek. They felt it best to go around Cyrus, the same way Japed had returned. They could then warn the caravan of the coming attack, which may endear them to the masters of the caravan again, and perhaps even reward them with the release of Hanna. Though it was a short journey around the mountain, it would be slow going with the sheep, taking them nearly two hours to arrive at the intended grassy hill.

The small company was ready just before the sun had set. Japed said a prayer of protection for their journey and forgiveness since they would be working prior to the end of the Shabbat. They knew time was critical. Cyrus was sure to take advantage of the darkness of these nights, possibly that very evening, and they both felt an urgency to be near the caravan.

CHAPTER 22

By Cover of Darkness

The Shabbat was coming to an end for the small caravan, and with the lack of chores, Hanna had thought long and hard of a plan to escape. She chastised herself for not leaving on the Shabbat. She knew that the party was unlikely to send someone to find her on such a day, but she had missed her opportunity. The wound in her heart festered throughout the day, keeping her from noticing that preparations were being made for one of the small wagons to carry the lords of the caravan to the town below them that evening.

It wasn't until Caleb had come to her with word that she would be accompanying the masters as an interpreter that she even realized what was occurring. He had given her some clean outer garments that were very beautiful and wouldn't smell of smoke from the cooking fire. He told her that all she needed to do was quietly sit in the rear of the wagon and be available if the masters needed her.

"Now don't speak unless you are spoken to first" he had said with a serious look in his eyes. "I will be leading the animals and will help you in and out of the wagon if need be, but will also be busy with my own tasks. There is word that the masters may be meeting someone very important tonight, maybe even the king himself."

With this news, Hanna's mind wandered as the master continued to give her instructions. "What if I meet the king and do or say something wrong", she thought to herself. "I am certain he will see that I loathe him or hear in my voice my hatred for what he and his leaders have done to my land."

Hanna's mind was a whirl, and before she realized it, she was sitting on a collection of soft pillows in the rear of the wagon. Around her were a number of the beautiful chests and items brought with the caravan, obviously gifts for whomever they were to meet.

She wondered why they would be visiting someone after the sun had set, and listening to the masters talking mostly in their own language was of little help. Yet, though they talked in quiet and somber tones, their excitement was obvious. As the small company rode into this beautiful town, with lights sparkling in the darkness, Hanna couldn't help but feel the excitement, yet had she known of the shadow following them, it would have quickly turned to fear.

Japed lead Joshua and the sheep along the small path that he had taken back to camp earlier, and away from the place he had met Cyrus. The two men had decided to stop for the night on the green hill just above the caravan, and that Joshua would go down to meet with them in the morning so as not to frighten them late in the evening. It would also give them a more advantageous point to show their intent as friends.

Joshua's heart raced at the thought of his seeing Hanna. And as they rounded the cliffs and came to the small grassy knoll where Joshua could easily see the caravan's cooking fire and tents below, he knew this was the same one he had spied out with Cyrus and Mahli nearly a month before.

"I believe this would be a good position for us tonight. It allows us to both see the caravan and to keep an eye on the area I met Cyrus" said Japed as he pointed towards the silhouette of the cliffs they had just avoided. "We should be out of his view here, but I believe it best that one of us be awake at all times just to make sure we're not surprised in our sleep."

"Well, my friend", said Joshua, "I'm not in the least sleepy, so you may as well get some rest while you can."

"That makes two of us", said Japed with anxiousness in his voice. "On our walk here, I thought much about the number of strange events that have taken us to this evening. Our meeting in the first place, your events with Cyrus and the caravan, not to mention Hanna's being taken by the same caravan and your running into Cyrus again. It would seem that the God of David was writing another story of intrigue through us."

"One would certainly wonder about all of these strange events. Though I see little of Jehovah's purpose in all of this, the challenges we've been through do remind me of the stories you told Hanna and me of our patriarchs. But I still can't understand why Jehovah allows innocent ones like Hanna to suffer, and the wicked, like our king and governors, and even that wretch Cyrus, to prosper?" Joshua had obviously been thinking hard on such issues and was coming to the realization that he had little control over the events of life.

"Yes, I too am uncertain as to why certain things occur, but I know that if our people had continued to serve Jehovah and one another as He commanded, we would not have allowed wicked leaders and the Romans to defeat, control or enslave us. But I have seen that when we become comfortable, we forget that we are not God, and when we do that, we become selfish and evil, like our King in Jerusalem. Then, to bring us back to goodness, Jehovah allows challenges to come in order to humble us and show us our need for Him." Japed seemed to be saying this as much for himself as he was for Joshua.

As the two men lay upon their mats, they pondered life and thought of the next day's events. They wondered if and how things would fall into place. Will there be another challenge thrust on them from the one who controlled the world? What if Hanna didn't want to come with them after all they had done to find her? What if the lords of this strange caravan had grown bitter against Joshua and force him to become a slave of theirs as well. Their minds raced through the endless possibilities of their next path of life.

Yet, all that they had been through and ever thought paled in comparison to what was to happen in the moments to follow.

CHAPTER 23

Glory!

As the two men thought on the events of the next day, they were startled by a sudden burst of pure white light that seemed to envelope them, as if the sun itself had fallen on the small hill. The suddenness of the light was blinding, and though both men jumped to their feet, neither could comprehend what had come upon them or where it had came from. Their first thought was that Cyrus had come upon them and surrounded them with an army of torches, but this light was brighter than any they had ever seen, completely disoriented their senses.

As their eyes began to adjust, they saw before them a man that seemed to personally emanate the light and dressed in pure white clothing, with light radiating from every part of his being and all about him. Though his hands carried no sword and seemed to be lifted towards the men in peace, the two shepherds were seized with terror and fell to the ground before the ominous vision.

The man then spoke to them with a powerful but beautiful voice that fell like a waterfall from all around, but with clarity like none they'd ever heard.

"Do not be afraid, for behold, I bring you good tidings of great joy that will be for all people. For unto you you born this day in the city of David a Savior, which is the Messiah and Lord. And this shall be a sign to you; that you shall find the babe wrapped in swaddling clothes and lying in a manger."

Joshua and Japed were completely alert and heard the words as if they were imprinted into their hearts, but were both to startled to fully comprehend the situation. And with irrepressible fear gripping their hearts, the two men fell to their faces, hiding their eyes from the ominous vision before them.

Suddenly, it was if as if the heavens themselves opened up and a company of people beyond counting were gathered all around the man, and everywhere they looked. Each was dressed in bright garments and singing praises to Jehovah: "Glory to God in the highest who brings peace to the earth and good will to all men."

It seemed like an eternity to the two men but also like no time at all. They remained stunned, lying face down on their mats long after the man and the company with him had faded into the night. Both too fearful and excited about what they had seen and heard to move.

"Did you see that?" Joshua finally asked in a quivering voice.

"I think I did", said Japed. "Was it an angel of God?"

"Meshugeh!" Joshua could hardly hold himself together. He was nervous and excited and scared all at the same time. "Why, why would Jehovah send us such a message? What was it he had said? Something about the Savior being born today in the 'City of David'? Where is that?"

"If I'm not mistaken, the city you see in the valley there below us would be Bethlehem; the City of King David. It's as if Jehovah

Himself has guided us here for this very reason. I believe we must do as the angel said and find this baby right away! Can you imagine?" exclaimed Japed as he began to shake with nervous excitement and an uncontrolled smile, "Jehovah Himself has given us a personal invitation to meet the Messiah of the world!"

"Then let's go right now! We can put the sheep together in that small inset in the cliff we passed with branches in front and should be in town in little more than two hours. But how will we know where the baby is?"

"If Jehovah is willing to open the heavens to us and give us this news, I'm certain He will lead us to the child." As Japed said this, Joshua was suddenly aware of the confidence in his companion and realized the quiet strength of this man he had come to love.

The two men prepared the sheep, and within an hour were well down the path towards Bethlehem, passing quietly by the caravan that they hoped held Hanna in comfort and peace. They discussed all that had happened, and though their excitement was almost uncontainable, they kept their minds about them as they quietly and quickly went on their way.

Hanna sat quietly in the wagon as their party rode through the dark evening towards the small town of Bethlehem. Though the pillows were soft, the ride still made Hanna's leg ache. Caleb had driven the wagon at a very slow pace in order to allow the masters time to decide on where they were to go, as well as to keep the noise of the company down. All the while, the masters continued to talk amongst themselves. To Hanna it seemed that they had uncertainty in the exact direction they were to go.

As the wagon rounded a crop of trees just within the town, out of the shadows crept a dark figure that brandished a glistening and much hated Roman gladius. The figure was upon them instantly and waived the sword towards the masters on their camels, and demanded the wagon to stop.

As the figure moved to the master, and held his sharp little sword against his side, the dark figure wickedly proclaimed, "So, my lord, it would seem that we once again have the privilege of meeting! Only this time, I not only will take the treasures you have so kindly loaded in the wagon, but I will also repay you for what you have done to my friend Mahli."

The master could barely see the figure in the dark of the night. The lanterns from the wagon were not adequate to show the details of their bandit, but the master instantly knew Cyrus' voice and wondered how long he had been following them in order to find them at such a disadvantage.

"So you have followed us all the way here just to steal what little treasure we have? What makes you think we are without guards?"

"No, my lord, but I've been watching and following you for some time now, and I'm certain that there are no others. You are careless to be carrying such a cargo without protection. But enough talk. All of you come down, or I will kill the master here." Cyrus was obviously accustomed to such a situation and pulled the master from his camel while continuing to hold the blade against his side.

The others had also come down from their own lofty rides, with one of the other Princes helping Hanna down from the wagon as well. The lanterns barely emanating sufficient light to see where to step, but the plenty to see the glint of the ominous Roman blade against the side of the master. Caleb, too, came around from the head of the mules, but his hand had carefully reached within his tunic for the small knife he carried within.

Caleb had lived through a hard life himself and knew what evil men thought. He knew he needed to wait for just the right moment or his master would lose his life, but he also knew that if he waited too long, it wouldn't matter to any since he was certain the thief wouldn't allow any to follow him. As he held to the handle of the blade, he came closer to the man.

"Good. Come over here against the wagon, all of you, so I can see you well," demanded Cyrus. Holding the blade against the master, he backed away slightly from the other four. Caleb positioned himself directly in front of the man and his captive.

A sound behind Cyrus caused him to shift his glance from the four against the wagon to look over his shoulder to a moving figure in the shadows. "Let them go!" He heard a gruff voice yell at him from the bushes nearby. "Let them go, now!"

While Cyrus' attention was drawn to his rear, Caleb pulled out the blade he was holding and stabbed hard at the arm that held the sword against his master, while pulling his master away from

Cyrus. With a yell, Cyrus let his sword arm drop for a second, but then quickly recovered and with his other hand, thrust the sword at Caleb stabbing deep into his stomach.

Instantly the shadow in the bushes and another from the right leapt into the dimly lit area and simultaneously grabbed Cyrus, with one thrusting a long slender blade deep into the back, and then the chest of the startled attacker. So it was, that in little more than the beat of his wicked heart, Cyrus fell dead to the ground.

CHAPTER 24

Death's Door and Heaven's Gate

Joshua and Japed stood there in silence, breathing hard, and looked down at the body of Cyrus. The chance of their coming upon the small company at just that moment had the adrenalin rushing through their bodies like pure energy.

It was Hanna who first caught the sight of Joshua standing before her. Her yell of surprise and jumping at Joshua caught him off guard as he tried to back away from this new attacker. But Hanna's voice calling out his name made him realize who it was, and he opened his arms to catch the young girl as she hurled her body towards him.

They held each other for only a moment until the groan of Caleb caught their attention. Hanna instantly released Joshua and lowered herself to Caleb's side. Her heroic guardian was panting for breath, bleeding from the deadly wound to his stomach.

"Caleb, Caleb" said Hanna in an anxious tone. "Hold on. Please hold on!"

The others gathered around Caleb as well, with Japed pulling the lantern down from the rear of the wagon so they could see their comrade. "Let's take a look at him", he said.

Hanna pulled Caleb's garments open in order to look at the wound. There was blood everywhere. Though breathing was not easy, he was able to talk. "It is all good", he said. "Please, my lords, please just put me in the wagon. Kamal will know what to do with my body."

"No, my friend, we will put you in the wagon and take you to a doctor in town here for healing". The master's voice was strong and reassuring. "You have saved my life and likely the lives of us all and we will make sure you live to tell the story to your people".

Hanna helped to tightly wrap some cloth around Caleb's abdomen, and the others lifted him carefully onto the pillows in the rear of the wagon. Each said a silent prayer for their friend and comrade as they carried him along and wondered if they would indeed find a doctor who could save him.

Joshua and Japed came again to Hanna and held her close. Hanna couldn't hold back the tears while the men didn't fight to keep their own from flowing as well. They held each other for several minutes before they heard the master say they needed to move soon in order to get care for Caleb.

So the company mounted the camels and loaded into the wagon. Joshua and Japed joined Hanna in the back near Caleb. The master came alongside the wagon.

"It would seem, my young master that I now owe you even more than I could easily pay. First, you warned us of this man and his companion's plans to rob us some time back, and now you have actually saved my life and even the lives of us all from this same evil man. How is it that you came upon us at just that moment?"

The master's voice gave a hint of both humility and concerned curiosity.

"In both instances, my lord, it was not by my planning but by Providence." As the wagon proceeded quickly towards the outskirts of Bethlehem, Joshua gave an account of how he and Japed had followed the caravan looking for Hanna. He told of how he himself had been stabbed by Cyrus a few nights before and how they came to be at the hill just above their caravan.

When Joshua and Japed gave the account of their visit by the angel, their excitement was proof enough to the reality of their story. All listened intently as they recounted the words the angel and the heavenly host had given to these two lowly men.

"Surely Jehovah has done this thing, and surely he is God over all gods" said another one of the masters. "And it is certain that he is no respecter of persons, for to us He has shown only pieces of a puzzle, to you He has shown Himself!"

"We ourselves are going into this town to find this King of which you speak. We have been following His star for many months now and have searched your ancient scriptures for an understanding of where we could find him. It was written long ago, from Micah your prophet saying 'But thou, Bethlehem-Ephrata, though you are little among the thousands of Judah, yet out of you shall He come forth unto me that is to be ruler in Israel; whose goings forth have been from of old, even from everlasting'. So you see, we are on the same quest, and not only did you save us these two times, but your information is also of great value to our purpose!"

In the back of the wagon, Caleb was struggling with consciousness. His breathing growing more labored with each step of the mule.

"Please hurry. I feel he has lost a lot of blood and is worsening". Hanna was holding his hand and wiping the sweat from his forehead with her sleeve. While she cared for his physical needs, she was begging for grace and mercy to the God of all things with all that was in her. And for the very first time, Hanna knew she was talking to the Creator of heaven and earth, and that He cared for His people, and more importantly, her.

CHAPTER 25

The Beginning

As the small caravan of travelers came into the city seeking a physician, they were astonished by activity this late in the evening. The town had been crowded with visitors due to the census, so most homes were busy and filled with visitors, many still walking the streets.

Just within the city walls, they found a small inn that seemed to be a center of activity for this outward edge of town, so Japed drove the wagon directly to the front of the inn, and stopping quickly, the master jumped from the wagon and hurried into the inn alone for information.

While Hanna cared for Caleb, the Masters shared more of their understanding of scriptures and writings from other lands of this coming King and what he would do. They said that the prophet Isaiah had written many things about the coming Messiah. About his being born of a virgin and being "God among men". That He would be called 'Wonderful Counselor, Warrior of God, The everlasting Father, and The Prince of Peace'."

At that moment, the master came rushing out from the inn, and with excitement in his voice, told them all of a young couple that because of the rooms all being taken in the area, were forced to stay in a nearby stall, and that the woman had delivered a son that very night. He said we would pass the stall on the way to the nearest doctor, less than a kilometer down this road.

The company was hopeful but worried. They could be within minutes of the Messiah, and yet minutes from possible life or death for their companion that lay at the back of the wagon. Hanna begged the masters to take Caleb to see the doctor, her eyes welling with tears as she pleaded for the life of her friend. Japed and Joshua had come around to see how the man was doing and to comfort Hanna.

"We do not have the money necessary to care for the man" said Japed, "or we could take him and find a doctor while you find the child. Maybe we could go by the stall and see if this is indeed the one we are here to see, and if it be Him, we will leave some to honor him, and others can take the wagon with this man to find a doctor."

All agreed to this strategy and hurriedly moved the wagon towards the stall the master was told of. In a few minutes they came before a little, secluded manger with a small fire in a pot and torch light just to the side. Inside the manger they saw a worn looking man standing over a beautiful young woman asleep, holding what appeared to be a new baby close to her on a bed of straw.

"Can I help you?" asked the man with a worried look on his face, as he came to the opening of the stall.

The three lords came forward and bowed themselves before the man. The master of the caravan spoke quietly but directly. "We are come from a far country in search of a child who would be born King of the Jews. Can you tell us truthfully, is this who we seek?" The sound of his own words seemed strange in his ears.

How is it that the King of all things and the Most High would be born in such a lowly place as this?

At this the woman awoke and pulled the baby near her for fear of those who had come to their small shelter. "Why do you ask?" she said.

"Blessed lady, please forgive our coming late in the evening as this, but we felt it best to find the child we seek by the cover of night. We are princes in our land and have followed the stars for these many days in order to find and worship the one that would be called Messiah. Please tell us the truth; do you know if this is He of whom we seek?"

The man by the woman's side looked down at the child and his mother, and in a solemn voice said, "This is He."

At the moment these words were spoken, Caleb cried out in pain, and stopped breathing, his body falling limp in the bottom of the wagon. Hanna reached for Caleb and called out his name, her voice startling all who were there. She cried out to him and shook him as if trying to wake him from sleep but to no avail. The pain she felt at the loss of her own parents flooded her mind, and she could do nothing but sob over this man she had grown to love. She held him close and prayed to God for his life.

With that, a strong gust of wind came whirling through the company that extinguished the torches and lanterns, and the babe lying alongside His mother awoke and began to cry.

Joshua heard Hanna cry out in pain the moment the lanterns had gone out. He moved closer to the rear of the wagon and reached out his hand to her. She seemed to be wreathing in pain herself. Joshua was frightened and didn't know what to do. He couldn't see anything but a silhouette of her tiny figure still holding onto to Caleb, rocking about in the bottom of the wagon.

Japed moved to the small fire that had been extinguished, and taking out a small burning stick went to light the torch. He then quickly moved to the wagon to light the lantern there, and when he did, he nearly dropped the torch to the ground at what he saw.

Hanna was now sitting up holding an alert and very much alive Caleb in her arms. Both were staring blankly at the lantern being held by Japed. But Japed was not as startled by his seeing Caleb alert and looking clear-eyed back at him, as he was with Hanna.

"Joshua, I feel strange" she said in a quivering voice. Though she didn't necessarily feel wrong, she felt little. Almost as if she didn't have any feeling at all. "Am I alright?"

Joshua came towards her, and taking the lantern from Japed, held it up close to Hanna. He reached his hand to her face. The scars that had been such a part of her for all the years he had known her were gone; her lips parting slightly in a look of concern were full and beautiful as she looked back at the man she had grown to love.

Joshua could tell it was Hanna, but not as he had ever seen her. There before him was a beautiful girl with a perfect face, sitting straight and strong. Even the fully alert Caleb, who she held in her arms, was looking up at her in surprise. Joshua put down the lantern and lifted Hanna from the wagon and set her on two strong legs.

Overcome by emotions, Joshua pulled her close to his chest and held her tightly for what seemed equal to all of the years of pain Hanna had lived through. Tears of joy were flowing freely down his cheeks. Then looking over at the babe that was now alert in his mother's arms, he took Hanna's hand and came to the mother and babe and laid himself down before them.

Without word, the others came along side and bowed themselves there before the couple and the child as well. Japed helping a healthy and whole Caleb down from the wagon also joined them at the feet of the young family.

"Blessed are you who have born such a one, and blessed be the King of kings!" said the master. Through Him, the world will be made whole, and by Him all will praise the salvation of Jehovah. With that, they presented unto Him gifts of gold, frankincense, and myrrh.

Joshua, turned toward his beautiful Hanna, and reaching over took her hand in his, and gave her a smile that only true freedom and love could give.

THE END

Daniel E. Wilson